GOOD DIFFERENT

MEG EDEN KUYATT

Schlolastic Press / New York

Library of Congress Cataloging-in-Publication Data
Names: Kuyatt, Meg Eden, author.
Title: Good different / Meg Eden Kuyatt.
Description: First edition. | New York : Scholastic Press, 2023. | Audience:
Ages 8–12. | Audience: Grades 4–6. | Summary: Seventh-grader Selah Godfrey
knows that to be "normal" she has to keep her feelings tightly controlled when
people are around, but after hitting a fellow student, she needs to figure out
just what makes her different—and why that is ok. Told in verse.
Identifiers: LCCN 2022035391 (print) | LCCN 2022035392 (ebook) |
ISBN 9781338816105 (hardcover) | ISBN 9781338816129 (ebook)
Subjects: LCSH: Neurodiversity—Juvenile fiction. | Self-actualization
(Psychology)—Juvenile fiction. | Self-perception—Juvenile fiction. | Self-control
in children—Juvenile fiction. | Emotions—Juvenile fiction. | Schools—Juvenile
fiction. | CYAC: Self-actualization (Psychology)—Fiction. | Self-perception—
Fiction. | Self-control—Fiction. | Emotions—Fiction. | Schools—Fiction. |
BISAC: JUVENILE FICTION / Neurodiversity | JUVENILE FICTION /
Social Themes / Friendship | LCGFT: Novels in verse.
Classification: LCC PZ7.1.K8946 Go 2023 (print) | LCC PZ7.1.K8946 (ebook) |
DDC 813.6 [Fic]—dc23/20220802
LC record available at https://lccn.loc.gov/2022035391
LC ebook record available at https://lccn.loc.gov/2022035392

10 9 8 7 6 5 4 3 2 1   23 24 25 26 27

Printed in Italy 183
First edition, March 2023
Book design by Cassy Price

For all folks on the spectrum, wherever you are—
you are loved and valued and worthy.

We have the power of dragons; therefore, we cannot live together with humans . . . we have the hearts of humans; therefore, we do not belong with monsters. We are outcasts in this world, never a part of either community. And so we live our lives alone, never to be understood by anyone.

—Myrrh, *Fire Emblem: The Sacred Stones*

The first time

I broke down
in front of anyone
was in the middle of the evil place:
Walmart.

All the people
and noise
pricked inside my head
like a hundred shirt tags.

It was a Saturday
and the aisles were crowded,
people yelled,
the overhead music crackled,
some smell like sour milk spilled
through the air and turned my stomach,
and Mom wanted me to decide
on a new pair of jeans
from the millions of racks.

All of a sudden
the whole store—
screaming kids
and stiff AC air—
was folding in on me,
like too-tight hugs from strangers.

I ran,
locked myself
in one of the changing stalls.
Mom banged on the door
but I balled up on the dirty
tile floor
and cried
and hyperventilated
till my head stopped spinning

and my eyes dried
enough for me to see.

When I opened the door,
Mom pulled me out
of the store,
ditching our groceries
by a mannequin
in reds, whites, and blues.

Once we got in the van,
she locked the doors.
She let me cry.
She opened the glove compartment
and gave me a pack of cookies.
"I always keep some goodies aside
for a bad day,"
she said.

But when I calmed down,
Mom said,
"Selah Godfrey,
never ever cry
in the middle of a store.

Always hold it in
till you make it back to the car."

That became
the first rule
for my list
on how to be
a Normal person.

For Mrs. V's Homework Assignment on Why I Like Pebblecreek Academy

by Selah Godfrey

Why do I like Pebblecreek?
It's a silly question. Of course
I like Pebblecreek. I just *do*.

I like the sound of the whole class reciting
the same jingle, or singing the same song, together.

I like learning words like "ubiquitous" and "omniscient"
that always surprise non-Pebblecreek adults.

I like the way my best friend Noelle wiggles her eyebrows
in that goofy Noelle way and makes me laugh
when we're in class or on cleanup duty.

I like that the stairwells always smell like Pebblecreek stairwells
and the classrooms always smell like Pebblecreek classrooms.

I like that I've been in the same school building ·
every year of school and know where all the rooms are.

At Pebblecreek, there's a way for doing everything:
raise your hand to speak in class
electronics off and put away
no makeup
lunches and jackets on the shelf
in your assigned spot
just outside the classroom.

Even though lots of kids complain
about all our rules, I like
that I don't have to think about
what to wear
and know what I'm
supposed to do.

3

Everyone at Pebblecreek is part of the Pebblecreek family,
and it really feels like that,
like all the teachers are my aunts and uncles
who always tell us at the end of each day,
"You are loved and worthy
and can do great things."

At Pebblecreek, all the kids invite each other
to each other's parties.
Even if we aren't all close
they're always *there*,
because we're stuck with each other
in the same classes each grade,
so we kind of have to get along.

I like that everyone knows me
as the Girl Who's Good at Drawing
and people always say nice things about my drawings
and ask me to draw them.

I like that there's a place for me at Pebblecreek.

Pebblecreek might not be perfect
but it's familiar
and I never want to change it,
like a pair of favorite shoes
that even if they're falling apart
you tape up and try to fix
because they're special and important
and yours.

Everything Wrong with Seventh Grade at Pebblecreek Academy

After the first week back, it's clear:
No matter what anyone says, it's nothing like sixth grade.
Sure, it's the same building I've always been in, but
    everything's rearranged since the summer.
There are new kids and teachers—everyone's crowded
    together like pencils in a pencil box.
I have to bump against desks to get out of our classroom.
Sometimes the AC stops working and Mr. Collins has to
    go outside on a ladder and fix it.
Our new uniforms make my skin feel poison-ivy itchy.
We have to tuck in our shirts even though it's hot and my
    skirt waist digs a deep burning ring in my skin.
Our homeroom teacher Mr. S is loud and thinks he's
    funny.
He keeps calling me SELL-UH instead of SAY-LUH, and
    stops class to make sure everyone knows that I'm
    doodling (why?).
He puts his foot on my desk every morning to show off
    his "socks of the day," and for the rest of the day, all
    I can think about are his shoe germs all over my
    desk (rude!).
We have a new principal whose smiles look fake like a
    party mask.
Noelle and I are in different classes, so we don't get to
    talk much except at lunch.
Mr. S seated me in front of Addie.
There aren't enough people signed up for Drawing 2
    so I have to take Drawing 1 again, which means
    sketching hands, and hands are so *boring*.
When school ends, the halls get crowded and loud and I
    have to push through people to get out, like some
    sweaty human ball pit.
But the worst thing is:
No one wants to talk about dragons.

Inside Me, There Are Dragons

When people ask me
what I want to do
when I get older,

I want to tell them
I'll become a dragon,
or a draconologist.

But I don't tell them that.
Obviously.

I made the mistake
of telling Mom once
and she said
I need to "get serious."

Because becoming a dragon
is not what adults call
a "viable career option."

Also,
dragons "don't exist"
(like that matters).

Online,
dragons are *real* and *alive*.
There are one billion, six hundred million search results
    for dragons.
There are elemental dragons
Pokémon dragons
Eastern dragons
Celtic dragons
cartoon dragons
How to Train Your Dragon dragons—
        In *How to Train Your Dragon*, there are Changewings,
        Scauldrons, Sand Wraiths, Shockjaws, Fastfins,
        Flightmares, and the Monstrous Nightmare (a Stoker

Class dragon), just to name a few, but my favorite species (obviously) is the Night Fury (obviously) because that's what Toothless is, and Toothless is the best character (obviously) because he's the main dragon and nice and powerful and one of the last of his kind, and all the Dragon Riders have their own dragons that are faithful companions who would fight to protect them and stick by their side *no matter what.*

Even though I have friends
and act like it's fine,
deep, deep down,
I really wish
somewhere
I could be fully *me,*
where I could relax
and not feel like a freak—

somewhere like Berk,
where I could have someone
fight by my side

like Toothless
with his Dragon Rider Hiccup.

Even If You Have Friends, You Can Feel Alone

At lunch I sit with the same girls
I've sat with since kindergarten.

My best friend Noelle loves fantasy books,
especially *Lord of the Rings*,
but it's not like
she wants to become an elf or anything,
so I only kind of talk to her
about dragons.
She might be *my* best friend
but she sits with lots of other people at lunch
and has lots of friends over at her house.
I don't know
if I'm *her* best friend.

Gemma is an easy friend
because she talks a lot,
so all I have to do is nod and smile.

Addie always says hi to me in the hallway,
always peers over my shoulder
during math class,
and breathes her annoying hot pizza breath
like a fire dragon
trying to break into the castle
of people's personal space.
She's less of a friend and more like
that person who's always at the lunch table
whether I like it or not.
But she's not mean like Cleo,
so I guess that counts for something.

Laurel puts notes
in everyone's desks,

saying things like
"You're beautiful"
or
"God loves you."

Today she gave me one that said
"You have a patient, congenial soul,"
so I'm pretty sure
she's just showing off
our latest English vocab words.

All of us are Pebblecreek Kids, meaning
we've been at this private school
since it started eight years ago
and we'll be here
until we die—
or at least graduate.

Pebblecreek is all
I've ever known for school,
and I'm fine with that.
Dragons don't like change.

But today at lunch
Cleo goes on about how cute
Matt from Class B is
and how she "accidentally" bumped into him
in the supply closet
and all the girls want to know the deets.

I'd rather talk about
myths or dragons
but keep that part of me
locked up
because I know the girls
don't want to talk about myths or dragons.

"I think Matt likes you," Laurel says.
Gemma squeals.
"Shut up!" Cleo says, but she's grinning
like she doesn't want anyone to actually shut up.
They all lean in close
and with the loud cafeteria noise
I can't hear. Not like I'm missing much.

At lunch, Noelle always saves a seat for me.
I'm here,
but also
I'm not.
I try to nod at the right parts
as Cleo and Gemma talk
but it feels like an ocean grows
between me and the other girls.

    "Did you see that video . . ."
                "I LOVE that one!"
      ". . . I can't believe Mr. S said that! He's so weird!"
"I *hate* piano practice . . ."
      "Did you see that girl randomly dancing outside?
      What a weirdo!"

Sometimes when they talk, I close my eyes
and imagine growing a tail
and hiding in the woods,
puffing out all the steam and smoke inside me
or flying until I find
a quiet island
with other dragons like me.

Sometimes when one of them calls me
and won't stop talking,
I turn my video off,
put my phone down,
and come back

and they're still talking
like they didn't even notice
I was gone.

My Normal-Person Mask

I can be really good
at pretending to be a Normal person.
This morning, I put on my Normal-person face.
I tucked in my shirt.
I said hi to the teachers who greeted me in the hall.
I smiled and nodded at all the right parts as Gemma
    talked before class.
I drew to keep myself distracted from
      all the rough noises and loud textures poking me.
I got a break in Mrs. V's nice quiet class, then pretended
    I could hear what the girls said in the loud cafeteria at
    lunch.
I looked my teachers in the eye when they called on me.
I stuffed my feelings into my chest like used tissues.

When my chest got full and raced with panic,
I asked to go to the bathroom and locked myself
in one of the stalls and studied the pattern
in the cinder-block bricks until I calmed down enough
    to go back.

Pretending to be a Normal person is tiring.
As soon as Mom pulls into the driveway
and I get inside, I change
    take off my Normal-person mask
    put on my headphones
    play my favorite pop songs on repeat.

I watch my favorite episode of *Riders of Berk*,
recite along with the characters,
laugh at all my favorite parts.
I squeeze my stress ball,
pluck the hairs that grow between my eyebrows,
flap my hands,
and don't care if it looks weird,

because no one is watching
and I have to recharge
at least enough
to do it all again tomorrow.

New Neighbors

Right before school started,
they moved into the old house next door.

I find broken beer bottles
on the border between our house and theirs.
In their driveway, there's a giant black stretch limo
half-covered in a tarp,
like it's a secret
they're really bad at keeping.

I don't know how many of them
live in that house
or what their names are
but there are a lot of them—
each time I look over, I see
different strangers
on the lawn,
different cars
clogging up the driveway.

Mom bakes them cookies,
but every time she tries
to bring them over,
they don't answer.

"They're probably not home,"
she keeps saying,
even though we can see
the lights on in their windows.

Mom

People say it's her blond curls
her naturally blushed cheeks
her blue eyes

but I think what makes
my mom beautiful
is the quiet lake
between her words,

how she doesn't need
to fill space
with sound or touch.

Talking with Pop is fun
but being with Mom
is like resting under
a calming tree.

Driving home from school,
she doesn't make me talk.
I can stare out the window
and imagine dragons
flying over houses and shopping centers.

Mom is *nothing* like me.
She understands people
and always has an answer
for what you should say
when
and why.
Mom's world makes sense.
It has *rules*.

Everything outside
our small corner of the world
is Alice-in-Wonderland chaos,
but Mom plows through it
effortlessly.

Mom never goes anywhere
without cookies in her purse,
is able to make
even rainy days
into something fun.

She's the one
who taught me how to draw.
She insists
she's not very good,
but upstairs in her office,
the walls and floor are covered
in her oil pastel faces:

self-portraits

my faces—
one for each year
of my life

and, behind a stack of canvases,
one of my dad's
clean-shaved face
before he left us.

Gaps

I don't know   what my dad likes to do,

if he likes to draw like me and Mom

      or ride bikes like Pop. I don't know

what he likes to eat   if he likes dragons

or if he'd sit   in the woods and talk to the trees

around our house   when he was upset

      like I do.

Mom doesn't talk about him much,   and I

    was too young to remember him.   Little

gaps of him sit   in the corners of our house:

the third chair   at the dining room table,

the walls   where the paint is darker

because there used to be things hung there,

the cut-out parts of old photos in our album

where all that's left of him   is the space

around his body.

         If I'm honest,

I don't think about him much.   Why would I?

You can't miss   someone you never knew.

At least that's what   I tell myself.

"It's Not That Loud," Which Means "Actually It's Really Loud"

The new neighbors
like to have loud parties.
I can hear them through my bedroom walls.

Even with my headphones
even with my door and windows closed
even with my volume turned all the way up
I can feel their music
like someone put their speakers in my chest.

Some nights I can't sleep,
my heart jumping
at every sound.

It's like the neighbors
are partying inside my head,
like they've picked the lock
to my body
and are walking inside me
with their muddy shoes.

It's the worst feeling in the world.

"They're not that loud," Mom says,
trying to smile, her voice
too bright. "Everyone has fun
in their own way."

But she keeps looking up
from her book
out toward their house.
When I go back to bed,   .
I hear her through the walls
sigh under her breath
and say to herself,
"You're doing great, Sue.

Everything is *fine*."

She says it like that: *fiiiine*.
I imagine her lips squished into a flat smile,
like dough stretched out by a rolling pin.

I hear Mom's heels
click on the hallway floor
going back and forth
across the house,
trying to get away
from their sound.

If Mom hates it too,
then why don't we say something?

Pop

Pop is Mom's dad
but you wouldn't know
from how they talk.

Mom smiles even when
I know she's sad,
but Pop says everything
going on in his brain
and you'd better try to keep up.

Pop's house is right next door
and smells like
old potpourri and antique malls.

When he smiles,
his eyes squint into little bird's feet.

He always wears
orange-tinted sunglasses,
always carries
the same notebook in his shirt pocket,
always bikes off
or wanders into the woods
deep in thought,
making Mom worry
because Pop never stays
in any place for too long.

Pop's the one person who gets me,
says "we're cut from the same cloth,"
like we're two matching button-down shirts
in the same closet
even though he's seventy-four
and I'm twelve.

But the best thing about Pop
is that he's always there for me,

that I don't have to try to translate
or worry if he's actually secretly
angry at me or not.

The best thing about Pop
is that he's 100% Pop.

All Out

Pop's only flaw
is that he loves Bob Evans
and insists we go
on Saturday morning.

I hate Bob Evans
and its always-greasy smell
and its food that makes my stomach turn over and over
      like clothes in a washing machine
and its eggs that have the wrong texture
and its screaming babies
and yakking old ladies
and the chatty waiters who somehow know my name
      and always try to talk to me.

Pop slides me his four-colored pen
like he always does
when I forget my own,
and I draw in my notebook
to disappear,

and like always,
Mom gives me that look,
her hushed
"*Selah.*"

I know I'm "too old"
to draw at restaurants,
but it's just Mom and Pop
and there's only so much Normal
I can be today
after all of last night's noise
still bouncing in my head,
and only so much
I can do
to survive a place
like Bob Evans.

Mom gets up
to use the bathroom,
and Pop leans over
his roast beef sandwich
and says to me,

"You know, kiddo,
when I'm feeling off,
I write it all out.
Might wanna give it
a try sometime,
see if it helps."

He pats the notebook
in his shirt pocket.

I shake my head.
"I draw it all out,"
I say,
trying to draw
a dragon shooting fire
at our neighbors' noisy house,
but I messed up the eyes
and there's no way to fix it
since it's drawn in pen.

I start over and draw
as hard and careful as I can
but I'm not sure I can say
I feel much better.

Rules to Being a "Normal" Person

Don't disagree with people or start conflicts (who knows
    what they might do).
Don't cry or make a scene in public (Mom only cries
    when she thinks I can't hear her).
Don't talk about dragons so much (the girls at lunch
    were quiet when I did).
If you can't say something nice, don't say anything at all
    (even if other people aren't always so nice).

If someone looks away while you're talking, stop (they're
    probably bored).
If someone doesn't get back to you, don't ask them about
    it (they probably don't want to see you).
If someone says it's fine, it may or may not actually be
    fine (it's the polite thing to say).
Always say you're "fine" (even if you aren't).

Smile (so no one mistakes you for being angry).
Wait to be invited to a friend's house (Mom says there's
    nothing worse than being an unwanted guest).
Wait for permission to go to the bathroom, or to do
    basically anything (it's rude to assume).
Don't give *anyone* a reason to think you're being rude
    (rude people are literally the *worst*).

Stay still in your seat.
Brush your hair.
Make eye contact.

        All the prickling and burning inside you
        is just stuff everyone else puts up with.

Even if your legs itch and you feel
hot and sweaty, if your heart races
from all the people in the room,
or your brain stops from having
to look in people's eyes,

and you want to scream
because everything feels too BIG inside you,

don't do anything that might draw
what Mom calls "undue attention"
(like Ezra, who's always being sent to the office
for doing something wrong).

Whatever you do,
always
be on your Best Behavior.
Follow the rules.
Otherwise, people will know
what you're *really* like
and who knows what they might do?

Even if the world
doesn't make sense
and things are scary
and unpredictable,
you can count on the rules
to make order
from the chaos
so that things can stay the same
and no one gets hurt
including
you.

Addie

At school on Monday,
Laurel's note reads:
"I have a feeling
something new and exciting
is going to happen today!"
I hope she's wrong.

Mr. S makes sure
the whole class knows
I got the only A
on the math test this week.
Everyone claps
like a thunderstorm
and I want to crawl
under my desk
but instead try to give
a Normal-girl smile.

On the way to lunch,
Addie stops me,
scrunches her face
all close to mine.
"Wow, you're so smart, Selah!
I didn't understand that test
at all. Do you think
you could go over it with me
so I understand? Mom'll kill me
if I fail another test."

I have no interest
in talking with Addie
more than I have to.
But if I said that,
it would probably
hurt her feelings
and sound mean.

There's nothing
wrong
with Addie, just that
she's always a little
too close
too loud
too smiley
and being around her
too long
is like staying out on the beach
without sunscreen
and coming home
with itchy red skin.

Her question
isn't a question.
The rules say
I have to say yes.
It would be rude
to say no.
She smiles
her fluorescent-bright smile.

As much as I want
to avoid Addie,
what would she do
if I said no?
Would she yell? Cry?
Ignore me? Say something
I don't understand?
Would a teacher like Mr. S get mad?
My chest thuds with panic
just thinking about it.

So I follow the rules,
and Addie and I
stay after school
with our test papers
while I try to explain

how to solve for X,
which is hard because
it seems pretty obvious
and also because
it's after school
and I'm low on words
and should be in my quiet room
in my soft home clothes.

At some point,
Addie says
in her stinky egg-salad breath
that this was great
and we should do it
again sometime.

And next thing I know,
Mom says it's great
how I offered to stay after school
every day
to help Addie
like the good friend I am.

When we get home,

I just barely
make it to my room
before crying.

All the words
and loud voices from the day
still scream through
a megaphone in my head,
the smells
and burning lights
etch into my brain.

I still feel
Addie invading
my personal space
like an army
firing trebuchets
at castle walls.

Why can't everything
just leave me
alone?

I've been wearing
my itchy school shirt
itchy feelings
itchy Normal mask
so long
it feels like my face
is gonna burn off.

Swimming

Noelle's family just got a pool,
so Noelle insists on swimming
when I come over after school.

I keep my swimsuit in my backpack,
knowing this, because otherwise
she'll try to con me
into wearing one of hers,
which is even worse.

After a long night of pretending
not to hear the neighbors,
and an even longer day
of helping Addie with equations,

I get in the water
slowly
and lie on my back
like a starfish.

It's only when
I feel the bracelet
Mom gave me for Christmas
slip off my wrist
that I realize I forgot
to take it off

and it sinks
to the bottom
of the pool.

"Oops,"
Noelle says for me.

I stare at it
through the water
like the water is
an impossible glass wall.

"Aren't you gonna get it?"
she asks.

Once, my mom
paid me
to put my head
under the water
to pass my swimming class.
But I've never made it
to the bottom of a pool.

I don't know what to say.
Is this something
everyone else can do?
That acid sting
of chlorine in your eyes
and nose and throat?
That unbearable
wetness all over your face?
That terrifying feeling
of not being able
to breathe or see,
like your body
is a flooded, sinking ship?

Noelle is a fish,
more underwater
than above it.
How does she do it?

When I don't move,
Noelle dives
into the deep end
and comes back
with my bracelet.

She looks me
in the eye—
through me—
like she can smell

my fear
through the biting chlorine.

But then she shrugs
as if to say,
Some people have weird quirks.
But whatever.
Let's swim.

I lay my bracelet at the edge of the pool,
then return to floating on my back.

We start talking and Noelle says,
"I don't get why Cleo's so obsessed
with Matt. It's like all
she'll talk about now. Laurel and Gemma
are always asking who I have a crush on
but I don't have any. I don't
want any. Maybe it's weird
but I don't think I like boys or girls
or anyone like that."

"That's not weird at all," I say,
feeling everything she's saying.
"Crushes are overrated."

Noelle smiles, climbs onto
the diving board,
and jumps in with a big splash.
It's moments like this
I feel like Noelle and I
aren't so different.

What if I told her
what I'm really like inside?
Would that make things weird?
What if Noelle
didn't understand
how the world presses in on me
and decided to stop being my friend?

I swallow my racing-hummingbird heart.
I can't risk her knowing.
I pinch my lips together
and keep my secret in my mouth.

For my thirteenth birthday, I get:

A pile of Bath & Body Works hand lotions
from Gemma, Addie, Laurel, and Cleo,
because Bath & Body Works hand lotion
is what you get people
when you have no idea what to get them.

A blue dress
that pinches my armpits
and makes me look
like a bloated blueberry
from Mom,
who says I could look like
a movie star
if I would just brush my hair
and dress up a little
(who cares
about movie stars?),

but also some tickets
to something called FantasyCon
and some new pastels.

A friendship key chain
shaped like a unicorn
from Noelle.

A new fantasy book
with a dragon on the cover
and a notebook
with Smaug on the front
("For your thoughts")
from Pop.

A gift card
to that clothing store at the mall
that all the girls in class talk about

from my dad.
It's tucked inside one of those cheesy
flowery greeting cards
he sends every year,
signed with nothing else written inside
to let me know what he thinks of me.

A new age—I'm technically
a teen—that everyone says
will be different and "fun."
No one asked me,
but if I had a choice,
I'd rather stay twelve.

The Worst Thing

To celebrate my birthday, Mom says I should go sleep over
at Noelle's tonight. Last night, we heard the neighbors
    laughing.
Screaming. She won't say it, but I know they were drunk.
    What I know
about drunk people is that they're even more
    unpredictable
than not-drunk people. So maybe it's good to not be
    home tonight. Maybe

the sleepover will be fun. Maybe in the late-night quiet
    dark of the sleepover,
I can tell Noelle about how annoying the neighbors are
and how I have trouble sleeping some nights
because all my brain can do is think about
how they're going to wake me up and freak me out.
How sometimes they make me so upset
I imagine being like Smaug, destroying the city of Dale.
It's a Tolkien reference, so maybe Noelle will understand.
Maybe I can say in the dark what I wouldn't say
out in the open. That's the magic of sleepovers.

But when I get over to Noelle's with my sleeping bag,
it isn't just Noelle. There are a bunch of girls
from our lunch table. Worst of all, there's Cleo,
worming her fingers all through a bowl of Cheetos.

When I turn around, Mom's already pulling out of the
    driveway.

Everything I Don't Like about Big Sleepover Parties

Or

Is This Supposed to Be Fun?

Cleo keeps turning the music up.
Everyone wants to stay up and dance even though it's one
    in the morning.
Addie keeps laughing and screaming at every joke.
And even though Noelle's mom comes down to tell us to
    be quiet, everyone's "quiet" volume still shoots Ping-
    Pong balls through my head.
Gemma wants to play Light as a Feather, Stiff as a Board,
    and have us all put our hands under her to make
    her float ("You too, Selah").
But Gemma isn't going to float, and her skin burns my
    fingers.
Even though I curl up in my sleeping bag, Addie keeps
    poking my face and asking, "Is she asleep?
    Is she *seriously* asleep already?"
Cleo searches on Netflix for some M-rated show, and
    every curse word stings like bees in the back of
    my ears.

But everyone else seems to be having fun—
what if I can't keep on my Normal-person mask
and say or do something I can never take back?

So I lock myself in the bathroom and huddle in the tub
bite my lips
try to hold in the panic
until Noelle comes to knock on the door
probably because she could hear me
crying through the wall.

When I Come Out

Everyone's quiet
for the rest of the night

No one says anything
about my crying

The TV is off
The music is off

Everyone curls
into their sleeping bags

turned away from me
like I'm a land mine

everyone's afraid
of setting off

On My Homework for Why I Like Pebblecreek

Mrs. V wrote a big check plus.
Then, at the bottom:
You're a good writer, Selah.

Stuck

Everywhere I go,
I can't get away from Addie.

She's a net, and I'm a fish—
no matter how much I try

to swim away, she always
catches me.

After school, Addie asks me
to explain variables and monomials *again*.

Even though we've done our hour,
she asks me, "Why were you crying

on Saturday? I thought we were all
having fun." Like it isn't obvious.

Is she just making fun of me?
When I don't say anything,

she scoots her desk next to my chair
until there's no gap between us.

"Whatcha been drawing?" she asks,
standing up, grabbing my notebook

and flipping through the pages. I try to scrunch in
like a turtle hiding in its shell.

They're not done, my thoughts loop.
They're not done, I can't get my mouth to say.

The latest drawing is just a dragon's mouth, open,
ready to breathe fire or cry or scream.

Addie's eyebrows scrunch, as if trying
to figure out what it is.

Is she trying to get on my nerves?
Why won't she just leave me alone?

She has to know how annoying she's being, right?
She has to know she's always invading my space.

But it'd be rude to tell her to back off.
Maybe she'd get angry, or complain to a teacher.

Maybe she'd just bug me more,
knowing she's succeeding in annoying me.

Even if I wanted to tell her off,
my mouth is empty.

I can't find words, only
my racing heartbeat

like I'm in the middle of battle,
and that sour morning-taste

like I might throw up
all over Addie and my desk.

Feelings

I overhear Cleo in the bathroom:
"I read online that people with autism
don't have feelings.
Do you think that's what Selah has?
Autism?"

                        "No way,"
                     Laurel says.
        "There's this kid at my church
                 who has autism
           and he can't talk or anything.
      Sometimes he flaps his hands
              and groans
             and it's scary."

      What's scary about someone who doesn't talk?
        What's scary about flapping your hands?

                "Yeah, no, Selah's weird
              but she's not, like,
               that weird,"
             Gemma adds.
         "If she had autism,
       would she even be able
            to go to school?"

"Of course she would."
Cleo's voice again.
"Autistic kids
are super smart, right?
At least
the *less bad* autistic ones are.
Like, they can remember anything.
They're basically human computers.
That's probably why
they can't feel emotions.

Computers can't feel anything either, obviously."

If only Cleo knew
just how many feelings I have
bubbling inside me like lava.

Be Reasonable

At lunch, Gemma says something like:
"I just don't understand
why people get so angry and violent.
Sure, the world isn't perfect
but maybe if they were reasonable,
we could all get along
and make the world a better place."

All the girls nod their heads
and bite into their Lunchables.

What Gemma doesn't know,
what none of the girls seem to know,
is that it's easy to be reasonable
when everything is fine.
When everyone thinks like you.
When you feel safe
and your bedroom is quiet.

It's easy to be reasonable
when you don't feel
every conversation in the cafeteria
banging to get into your brain,
or all the tangled smells of packed lunches
make your stomach turn with nausea,

when every loud noise doesn't feel
like a knife in your chest,
and the biggest thing you have to complain about
is Mr. Blaire's grading on the logic test.

I've been trying to be reasonable,
but I feel my Normal mask
starting to crack. Would that really be worse,
unreasonable,
than always being scared,
always holding
all the bad feelings in?

Half an Hour before School Lets Out:

Sometimes I feel like
I'm going to burst open

the dragon inside me
hatching from its egg.

The Incident

Study hall is supposed to be quiet,
a break
from all the noise and talking
to work on homework
or draw
or just sit and think.

But the other kids are loud,
throwing heavy words
around the room
like anvils. Even if I don't want
to listen to their conversations,
my ears attach to every word
like magnets,

and the heavy words settle
into my forehead
until they shape into
a massive headache.

I try to hide in drawing.
I try to keep my mouth shut
and be "the good kid" people think I am.

But the busy halls
and hot, crowded room
and the memory of the rude neighbors
and the warm, itchy uniform
and the squeaking dry-erase markers
poke at me like thumbtacks
all the time
and I'm sick of it.

I tell myself
to push it all inside
until I can get home.

Then Addie leans over behind me
and starts braiding my hair.

Why?

I suddenly feel her fingers in my hair
like electric spiders
crawling and pinching
and taking over my whole head.
She doesn't even ask first or anything.

I can't think,
I can't gather words.
My body takes over.
I scream and turn
and my arm moves without me thinking,
hitting her
like she's a fly buzzing around my head.

But my hit
is too hard.
Blood runs out
Addie's nose,

and the whole room goes still.

Blood

drips from Addie
onto the tile floor.

Blood is supposed to be
in your body,
not outside it.

I've never had
a bloody nose,

but the way Addie
bites her lip,
scrunches her eyes,

I can tell
I did a terrible thing,

the worst thing,
the thing all my rules
try to protect me from doing:

making
someone

hurt.

Worst Nightmare

Everyone stops talking.
The chess boys stop playing chess.
Mr. S stops grading papers.

Everyone's eyes
are on me,
I can feel them
like slime:

the confusion
disgust
and worst of all
the fear
I might do it again.

Waiting

Sitting downstairs
in the school office
waiting for Mom to come,

I'm some exotic
zoo animal.

Mrs. Tucker
has propped open the doors
so everyone sees me
on their way to PE,
funneling into the gym
in their blue shorts.

Addie isn't there
(obviously).

Everyone's eyes
stick on me
like those sticky toy balls you get
in dentist office vending machines.

Ezra glares at me
like he's trying to shoot
laser beams across the hall
through me.

I imagine
cage bars
in the doorway,
made to protect
zoo guests
from me

but also
to protect me
from zoo guests.

Principal Merkert's office

used to be a closet.
My sixth-grade classroom
was the old principal's office,
but as the school gets bigger,
rooms are running out.

I've never had
to be here before.
I'm not the kind of kid
who breaks the rules.

There's just enough space
for him to get behind
his desk,
and for Mom to squeeze
into the corner
across from him.
I sit by the door
so I can feel less
like I'm being buried alive.

Principal Merkert
tries to put on
his smiling Santa face,
stroking his pepper-gray beard,
but my chest still feels like
horses are racing inside me,
and Mom doesn't even wear
her Polite smile.

Principal Merkert says things like:
in accordance with the code of conduct
in the school handbook,
she'll be suspended for three days . . .
zero tolerance . . .
warning . . .

when she gets back, we'll need to see
her Pebblecreek best . . .
decide if we can invite her back
next year . . .
but I can't focus. My head,
the whole office
is spinning.

Principal Merkert turns to me.
"We'd hate to have to
ask you to leave, Sarah.
We love
having you at Pebblecreek.
But we can't have something like this
ever
happen again."

I tell him my name is Selah.

Pebblecreek Academy
used to be small enough
that everyone knew
each other's names.
But now it feels different,
tight,
like a shirt
that shrunk in the wash
and makes your arms all itchy.

"There won't be
a next time," Mom says. "There won't be
any more problems."

Not Knowing

Mom's quiet
as we walk out of Pebblecreek
to the car.

She's quiet
as we drive
out of the parking lot.

She only speaks
when we pull up
to the house.

"It's just so
unlike you,
Selah."

I look down
at my hands
and hope she's right,

because some days
I have no idea
what is or isn't me.

The Talk

"You aren't supposed
to hit people," Mom says.
"Period.
You *know* this."

I know.
I wish more than anything
I never hit Addie.

But what do I do
about the fire
inside my body
that just keeps getting
bigger and bigger?

I want to tell Mom this,
but keep my lips
sealed
like a ziplock bag.

Keep the fire contained
no matter what.
Another rule
for my Normal list.

"Just one more problem
and they can expel you,"
Mom says, every muscle
in her face tight.

Mom works hard
to pay for Pebblecreek's tuition.
I'm one of the Pebblecreek Kids.
But now I'm also the Girl Who Hits People.
What would she do if they expelled me?
Where would she bring me?
Somewhere

with long, strange hallways
and classrooms I've never seen.

Somewhere without Mrs. V
or Noelle
or anyone I know.

I can't risk
messing up again.

But a small voice inside me
can't help but ask:
What if I explode again?
What if I hurt someone else?
What if it gets worse
and worse
until I become
all dragon
no girl
and set fire
to my life?

Pop comes over for dinner,

doesn't wait for Mom
to open the door,
doesn't knock,
just comes right in
like he always does
on dinner nights.
If it was anyone but Pop
this would feel intrusive—
rude—
but it's Pop.

"Well, hey there, kiddo,"
he says,
"what'cha making this time?"
and I look up
from my half-started sketch
of a dragon's eye
and try to smile,

but Mom is burying
her face in the stove-top steam.
No smiles.

"You gonna tell me what's wrong?"
he asks.

Mom tells him,
"Selah hit a classmate,"

and Pop shrugs.
"OK."

Mom and Pop in the Kitchen

OK? Dad, I don't think you understand.
You can't just tell your granddaughter
it's OK to hit people.

> I don't recommend hitting people
> as a general rule, but there must be
> a reason Selah did it.

There's *never* a good reason to hit people.

> Maybe not a good reason,
> but there's always a *reason*.
> Everyone gets upset sometimes.

Dad, they could *expel* her for this.

> If that hoity-toity school
> would expel a kid like Selah
> over one small thing like this,
> they probably aren't that great a school to begin with.

One small—
Dad, why do you do always this?

> Do what?

Never mind.
Let's talk
about something else.
How was your bike ride—

> No.
> This is important.

                                        If they try to expel Selah,
                        I'm gonna walk right down there and—

Dad. You are *not*
doing that.
Look, how about you give me
a couple minutes
to finish dinner . . .

                                        All I'm saying is
                        people make too much of a fuss
                        over folks who are different.

Burst

Mom
slams
a bag of noodles
on the counter
so hard
it breaks open
and all these little
pasta bits
confetti on the floor.

I jump in my seat.
Her voice
is loud,
louder
than I've ever heard
before. Louder
than the rules say
you should ever speak.

"*I* am the parent here.
I will decide what's best for Selah.
Keep poking me
and things'll get ugly."

Mom holds her chin up
but I see her hands shake.
Why? Pop is trying to help.

If my dad was here
and Mom wasn't the only parent,
what would he say?
Would he be upset like Mom?
Would they argue too?

She bends down
to pick up
the broken pasta pieces

and I get up
from my chair
to help her.

Pop looks
as confused
as I feel
but he nods and says,
"Of course, Sue."

Dinner

is quiet.
Pop slurps his Alfredo noodles.
Mom takes small bites
smearing red lipstick
on the edge of her fork.
She tries to get us talking
but my thoughts
are nowhere near this table.

Addie covered her face
as she went to the office
but we could all
hear her cry.

I made her cry.

How is Addie?
Is her nose better?
I should apologize
but how am I supposed to
show my face
in front of her again?

I'm no different
than my rude neighbors.
Maybe the girls at the sleepover
were right to tiptoe around me.
What if I *am* a time bomb,
if I make everyone angry
like Pop made Mom tonight?
What if it's not OK
to be a dragon?

When I tell Pop why it happened, he says

"I don't care
what your mother's told you.
We live
in a weird world,
one not built
for folks like us.

If I've learned something
in my time on this earth,
it's that if you don't
stand up for yourself,
no one else will.

If I don't give my two cents,
no one will ask for it,
and it'll sit inside me,
boiling over.

So that's why I yap
and yammer
and write in my notebook.

Say, have you given that notebook
I gave you for your birthday
a spin yet?
If not, try it. Write
what really happened at school

and let it all out."

Pop Pats My Shoulder

"You know, kiddo
we dance
to the rhythm
of our own drums,
don't we?
We're cut
from the same cloth.

But you know what?
We'll
make
it
through
just
fine."

Folks Like Us

So it's not just me
feeling that bonfire in my gut?
Pop feels it too?

In the middle of the night,

I wake up to a scream.
I look out my window
and see a giant bonfire
like a blast from a Red Death dragon
in the new neighbors' lawn.
It's almost as tall
as their house—
isn't that illegal?

The flickering orange light
eating the pitch-black dark
makes my heart shake
my whole body awake,
like the fire is going
to eat our lawn, our house, me.

The shadow of a person
flickers in our yard.
Are they coming
to set our house on fire?

The person walks toward the neighbors' house.
The balding head.
The orange glasses.

It's Pop!

He walks up
to the bonfire crowd,
and I can't hear what he says,
but his whole body shakes,
his fists raised,
his steps big and angry.
Maybe he'll beat them up
or turn them in to the police
so I can finally get some sleep.

Thank you, Pop!

Someone stands up
from around the bonfire
and I can hear his yelling
all the way from here.

I get out of bed,
anger firing
in all my body's circuits.

But then a hand
clamps on my shoulder.
Mom in her pink bathrobe,
her lips pressed tight,
shaking.

"Don't you dare
go out there,"
she says,
then slips past me
into the night.

From the window,
I watch her grab Pop,
her body apologizing
to the rude neighbors.

Pop breaks from her grip
because nothing stops Pop,
not even Mom. Not even
Normal-people rules.
He keeps yelling
and yelling until
all the yelling is out of him.

Then he kicks dirt on the bonfire
and walks back to his house.

Mom comes back inside,
the bottom of her pink robe brown.
Locks the door.
Rubs her red eyes
like she thinks I can't see.

First Day of Suspension

I thought it'd be nice
to not be at school
but it only reminds me
how I broke my rules
and makes me
count the days
till I can go back
and prove to everyone
that I *am* a Good Pebblecreek Kid.

Pop's Treasure Hoard

If Pop is a dragon,
his basement is his treasure hoard.

He has all sorts of bikes and old train parts
and travel magazines from a hundred years ago

in piles you have to dig through to find
exactly what you're looking for.

When Mom leaves for work,
Pop brings me through his garage

to his basement shop,
and I know this means he trusts me

because no one shows potential thieves
their treasure hoard.

Pop shows me a steam whistle
that was on a B&O train in the 1890s.

A rusted carriage lamp
from a Union Carbide train.

A greasy fork
from the Elgin bike

he rode as a paperboy
in the 1960s.

"Some people think this stuff is junk,"
he says. "But this is gold to me."

Pop turns on his model trains
and I imagine riding a train

from one end of the country
to the other. Biking down a big, steep hill

and feeling the incredible rush

of wind in my face.

Pop and I are the same
in lots of ways.

We're both itching
to be in our own world.

The next day,

one of Pop's bikes is gone.
It's the new neighbors, I'm sure,
but Mom says it's better—
safer—
to just stay quiet.
That if we say anything,
it'll just get worse.
That Pop shouldn't have
gone over there
in the first place.

"But he was just saying
what we're all thinking,"
I tell her.
"He was trying to help,
and besides, what if
they don't stop?
What if they just keep being
loud and obnoxious?"

Mom shakes her head.
"Who knows what
those kids'll do.
They get riled up, it might be
more than a bike next time.
We can put up
with a little noise,"

she says,
closing all the curtains—
as if this can keep
the bad neighbors away.

When it starts to get dark,
I hear her go through the house,
double-checking all the doors are locked.

Dentist

I hate that me being suspended means I have plenty of time
    to go to the dentist.
I hate going to the dentist (who doesn't?).
I hate waiting in the waiting room and sitting in the hard
    chairs.
I hate the sound of ten different televisions playing
    different kids' films.
I hate how my ears try to follow each one and get them
    tangled in my head.
I hate the dentist's candy-coated voice as she comes to the
    lobby to get me,
        how she asks me how I'm doing,
        how the rules say I have to say "good"
        even though I'm obviously *not* "good"—
        I'm at the dentist after all.
I hate the grating sound of her scraping off plaque.
I hate the taste of marshmallow fluoride and blood.
I hate the smell of other people's mouths.
I hate the sting and ache of her poking at my gums.
      It's like a thousand bees stinging inside my mouth,
      like she's trying to chip out my teeth
      one by one.

But the thing I hate most of all
is how she'll stop
when I start crying,
her eyebrows scrunched
in worry and pity.

"It shouldn't hurt this much, Selah,"
she says. "It shouldn't hurt at all."

On the car ride home,

Mom says there's nothing wrong with me.
Some people are just more sensitive than others.
"Who likes the dentist? *No one.* Of *course* it hurts.
They're poking all in your mouth, for Pete's sake!
Can't she hear the kids screaming in the other rooms?"

Mom says everyone feels weird in seventh grade.
Your body is changing, you're not quite
a kid anymore but not 100% a teen yet either.
You're in the middle of lots of changes
and changes are hard.

But when Mom was my age, did she feel
like a dragon dressing up as a human?
Sometimes I feel like I'm an Amazon package
that was mailed to the wrong planet.
Even Pop said the world's not built
for folks like us.
Folks like him and me?
Folks like Mom and me?

But if that's true, that we're different,
then why won't Mom say it?

Mom turns right instead of going straight home.
She pulls into the parking lot
of my favorite art shop.

"I think today calls for a treat,"
Mom says, smiling at me
like I'm the most Normal human girl in the world.

Bad Actor

Sick
Cough
Groan
Sore throat
I don't think
I can go back
to school
yet.

Mom doesn't buy it.

No More Problems

"No more problems, OK?"
Mom says
as she drops me off at school.
"I know you can do it."

Ha.
Easy for her to say.

Like Mom knows anything
about what it's like
for normal to not come easy.

Coming Back after Suspension

The teachers who usually say hi to me in the morning
    look away
There's no nice note from Laurel in my desk
Gemma stops talking when I sit down

Cleo says, "You always have to watch out for the
    quiet ones."
Ezra says, "Why did they let *you* back here?"
If only I'd hit him instead of Addie

Mr. S uses Will's desk to show off his socks instead of mine
At lunch, Cleo makes sure there's no room for me at the
    girls' table
When people have to talk to me, they try to smile

But the worst part of it all
is how Addie looks at me
like I'm a wild dog that might bite off her legs

Cleanup

After lunch, everyone helps
clean up the school.
This is because Pebblecreek
can't afford janitors
and also
it "builds character" or something.

Noelle and I are on trash duty.
We tie up trash bags and walk
to the dumpsters out back.

"So what really happened?" Noelle asks,

and I feel my chest open up.
No one else has asked.
I tell her about Addie
and my hair
and the neighbors
and how everything's been
building up
and I exploded.

Noelle nods.
A pause.
"I mean
that's really weird
but like . . .
that's it?"

We stop.

"I mean,
yeah, Addie can be
annoying
and loud neighbors can be
annoying
but . . .

I guess I thought
if you hit her
it was something, like,
really bad."

I ask:

What has to happen
to make something
officially
"really bad"?

Trash Bag

I swing the trash bag
and throw it into
the dumpster-mouth
as hard as I can,

but it hits the metal lip
and rips,
smelly trash
pouring out its side.

Noelle's eyes widen.
She doesn't answer
my question. She looks
away, like she can't wait

to get away from
a weirdo like me.

I don't want
to blow up at Noelle.
I don't want
to blow up ever again.

But I'm like
that ripping trash bag,
and all that smelly stuff
is coming out,

showing just how strange
I really am on the inside
and who wants to hang out
with a smelly bag of trash for a friend?

Going Inside

Noelle and I
don't say anything
the whole way back.

It's not that
I don't want to say anything
but that
everything I can think to say
will only make things worse.

Besides, my worst
nightmare
was right:
My secret's out,
and I'm sure Noelle
doesn't want to hang out
with a weirdo like me.
Can I blame her? What if I hurt her
like I hurt Addie?

Dragons can be
solitary creatures
if we need to be.
Safer
for everyone
if we stay
in dungeons and caves
away
from everyone else.

Since there are no caves
at Pebblecreek,
I hide in paper,
pull out the notebook Pop gave me
and let all the words
I can't say
pour

out

on

the

page.

It goes without saying

that Addie isn't there
after school
in the multipurpose room
waiting for me
to help her with math.

Mom is outside in the van
ready to bring me home
and it's weird but
part of me wishes
I had a reason
to stay after school
and talk with Addie.

No More Jokes

Mr. S stops class.
"It looks like SELL-uh's drawing again," he tells everyone.
I don't correct him that I'm writing.
(I should write about Mr. S
and how he still can't say my name right.)
"Am I really that boring, SELL-uh?"
he says, no more joke in his voice.
"It's very disrespectful to draw in class."

I don't want to be rude.
Drawing actually helps me focus.
But I don't tell Mr. S that.
Not like he'd care.

"If I see you goofing off in my class
one more time,
I'm going to take all your pencils," he says.
My body gets tight.
My heart jumps up my throat.
Why do I keep finding ways
to do things wrong?
Mr. S looks at me
like I stole his socks-of-the-day.
I'm no longer
just a quiet kid to tease
but something scary to him
like a loud, barking dog
pushing through a chain-link fence.

In the back of the room,
Laurel raises her hand and asks,
"How is she supposed to take notes
or do homework
without a pencil?"

The whole classroom squirms
in the silence. No laughs

today. "Well," Mr. S mutters,
"let's just not have
any more doodling in here." He moves on
but the classroom still feels chilly,
chillier
than it should in October.

I write a thank-you note

and slip it onto Laurel's desk

between classes.

She doesn't write

anything back.

Rules to Being a Dragon

Do whatever it takes to survive seventh grade:

live in a lonely mountain cave
with your notebook and words.

There can't be problems
if you hide away and do your work.

Be as quiet as you can
when you fly from class to class. Sleep

with your back arched, ready to fight
because your species is endangered—

you're the only dragon
in a world built for people. Be careful

even with your friends. You never know
who might be carrying pitchforks.

So even if it stinks,
there's nothing you can do

but to try to blend in
and do your best to look like

what everyone wants you to be:
nice.
polite.
happy.
quiet.

Normal.
A good
little human.

Homework Poem

For homework, Mrs. V wants us
to write a poem. In my desk,
I have Pop's gift: my writing
notebook. It's filling up with scribbles
of feelings, not-really
poems. He keeps telling me
to write, but I'm not sure—
what exactly *is* a poem?
My feelings are loud. Rude.
BIG. Sometimes
angry. Are those OK in poems?
That's why I've kept them closed
in my mouth after all. Head
down. Don't
raise my hand or talk
in class. Don't make things worse.
People already want me
to disappear. Just remember
what Principal Merkert said.
One mistake, and I'm gone.
I can't write a poem that gives
anyone a reason for another
suspension or worse.
Will Mrs. V be angry?
Confused? Worried?
Noelle didn't get it when
I tried to explain my feelings. Writing
is for *me*. Pop calls it
making steam holes to keep us
from boiling over.
Is *this* even a poem?
If only Pop could write
my poem for me. But I know he'd say

something like, "Selah, you can do it.
There's no wrong way to write a poem."
Besides, I'll get in trouble
if I don't turn anything in at all.

Dragon-Girl

by Selah Godfrey

In my notebook, I love to draw
eyes.

Once Cleo opened my sketchbook
(without my permission, I might add)

and found the pages covered in eyes
and called it "creepy."

Eyes are powerful and terrifying.
Feelings pour out from them like a geyser.

People's feelings are complicated.
The things that come out of people's eyes

are things I can't always translate.
I can only look at them for so long without panicking.

But dragons are different.
Dragons don't say one thing and mean another.

Dragons don't have petty social rituals
over wearing specific brands of sneakers.

If a dragon doesn't like you, you know it because
you're probably dead.

There are dragons that shoot fire out of their mouths.
There are dragons that have wings and can fly anywhere in the
world.

A dragon doesn't have to let anyone ride it.
A dragon doesn't have to go to school.

A dragon doesn't have to do anything it doesn't want to.
If a dragon is scared, or angry, or surrounded by enemies,
it will attack.

It will break all the windows. Catch things on fire.
Fly through the wall and find a safe place to retreat.

But as much as I want to be,
I am not a dragon.

Maybe that's why I hit Addie.
It was the most dragon-like thing I could do.

In the margin of my homework poem,

Mrs. V writes lots of notes
but my favorite is:
"Sometimes I wish I were a dragon too."

More Poems

It turns out
I like writing poems.
They're like popcorn.
You eat a handful and then
you eat another handful.

When I write poems,
anything can happen.
Like maybe now
a dragon sweeps through
the window of my classroom
and swings its tail
to knock through all the walls
and rustle the desks like papers.
And school is canceled for forever.
I mean, I can dream, right?

When I write poems,
Mrs. V listens
and makes me feel like
what I think matters,
which makes me want
to write even more poems.

I write through class in the margins of my notes.
I write in the spaces between my dragon drawings.
I don't look up when people call my name.
I don't get up for lunch or recess.
I eat at my desk: sandwich in one hand,
writing with the other.
I write while waiting outside for Mom to pick me up.

I write so I don't have to think about
the looks people give me
what to say and not say
Noelle's sympathy waves
Addie

Ezra calling me Killer Robot
the way kids cluster
     away from me
     outside the parking lot after school
Or how Principal Merkert
     stands outside my classroom
     watching me
     reminding me
     if I get in trouble again
     I'll have to leave Pebblecreek
     forever.

I write and write
until I get to the end of a feeling
and feel the steam
inside me
go out through my pen
out the classroom
out the window
away into the sky.

On my way from the bathroom,

I hear voices in the main office.
Not quite yelling but sharp enough
to hit my ears.

"What do you think
you're saying, letting
that girl stay here?

All the parents know
what she did. How can we feel
that our kids are safe?

How can we know she won't
do something again?
Something worse?

My daughter says
that girl's always been strange.
Not playing

with the other kids at recess,
hiding in the bathroom
at sleepovers.

What if something's really
wrong
with her? How can you know?"

Wrong

I go back
    to the bathroom

lock myself
    in the far-most stall

and breathe in
    and out
        and in and out

and in and out and in until I'm no longer breathing but
panting like a hunted deer I can't stop I can't stop I'm
going to die I'm screaming I'm glad no one else is in the
bathroom Hope no one can hear me through the walls
Hope no one is afraid I might hurt them

I was right the rules were right no one wants the real
Selah inside just the bootleg imitation of a girl she
pretended to be

Because everyone says it
I'm not just different

Something is *wrong* with me

Breathing

Eventually
I start breathing again.
I study the pattern
of the bathroom tiles.

The bell rings.
English class is over,
which stinks
because I like reading time
and the soft Enya music
Mrs. V plays while we work.

The bathroom door opens.
"Selah?"

Under the stall, I see
Mrs. V's purple heels.

I take a deep breath,
unlock the door,
but before I can get myself to move,
I break out crying. Again.

Walk

Mrs. V offers to bring me down to the office
so my mom can pick me up early.
I shake my head.
Too much to explain.

"Well," Mrs. V says, "I have
an open grading period next.
Maybe we can take
a quick walk around the building?
That always helps me
when I feel upset."

We step outside
onto the quiet blacktop
beside the empty recess field
and walk around the building.
All the shuffles and voices
from inside feel
a million miles away.

Mrs. V asks me
why hitting Addie
made me feel like a dragon,
and I tell her I know
it was wrong, but it was
the only way I knew
how to say
what I needed.

Mrs. V asks me
what happened today, and I tell her
nobody wants me here
at Pebblecreek anymore.

"Well, that's not true," Mrs. V says.
"*I* want you here.
How else will I get to read

your lovely writing?"

I shake my head. Mrs. V
doesn't count. She's too nice
to hate anyone.

Secret

"I've been keeping a secret, Mrs. V.
I'm not like everyone else."

Mrs. V smiles.
"No one is like anyone else."

"No, I mean there's something
wrong with me.
I don't *want* to hurt people
but everything hurts me.
And I keep trying to follow
all the rules, but—"

"What rules, Selah?"

"The rules to being Normal."

"Like what?"

"You know.
Not bothering people.
Stuff like that."

"Like what?"

"Like . . .
Don't talk about dragons
because most people
don't care about dragons.
Don't get upset in public
or talk loud
or ask people
to turn the volume down
because they're enjoying it after all
and it's only you
that's getting upset.

Normal people
don't get bothered
by small stuff
like that."

But Aren't They?

"Selah,

sometimes
we make up rules
to try to make sense
of the world around us,

but those rules
aren't fair
to us
or anyone else.

Those rules
aren't real."

Being Normal, according to Mrs. V

"I don't like the word
'wrong'
being used the same way
as 'different.'

'Wrong' should be used
when we're talking about
morals,
not when we're trying to blend in
with everyone else.

I know
you weren't trying to hurt Addie.
Sounds like your body
was trying to protect you.
But there are other
. better
ways to protect yourself.

Talking to your doctor,
learning more about your needs,
communicating them—
those are all good things to do.
People can't help you
if they don't even know you need help.

You may have different needs
than some folks in your class,
but that doesn't make you the 'wrong' version
and other people the 'normal' version.
You are *Selah*.
And you are *not* the only one
feeling these things."

I Don't Know

Mrs. V and I go back inside.
She says she can write a pass
so I don't have to go
to my next class
and instead
I can stay in her office
and write poems.

I nod,
but my brain
is still swirling
with thoughts.

Even if Mrs. V says
the rules aren't real,
they still *feel* real.
I still feel them
binding my chest,
locking my thoughts
inside me. Keeping
the dragon inside me
from burning
everything
to the ground.

Without my rules,

how am I supposed to act?
What is
what isn't
OK?

I'm like milk
floating in outer space
without my rules.

I need some boundary
between me
and everything else

because, like milk,
either I'll spill over
everything around me

or everything around me
will spill into me
until I burst.

I need to make sense
of this strange, scary world.
I *need* my rules—

don't I?

If other people
don't have my rules,
how do they keep from floating?

Pop says
there are folks like us
but where are they?

And how do they keep
from floating out
into the middle of the sky?

Noelle

At lunch, I see Noelle
hover outside the classroom door.

"What are you doing up here?" I ask,
my stomach filled
with birds. Happy birds. Hopeful birds.
Confused birds. Nervous birds.

"I should be asking you," Noelle says.
"No one wants to eat up here, alone."

How would she know? It's not like
she's said anything about our dumpster
conversation. Like she's tried
to understand me. Before
I can stop myself, the words
shoot out like fire breath:

"Maybe I
want
to be
alone."

Noelle's eyes widen. She pulls
a scrunched-up envelope
out of her pocket.

"OK, then," she says, her voice
short. She slides
the crumpled envelope on my desk,
holds her chin up.
"So . . . I'm having a party
if you want to come."

Noelle always invites
all the girls in our grade
to her birthday party.
She's just trying to be polite.

Her mom probably made her invite me.

When I say nothing, Noelle
shifts on her feet. "Well,"
she says, "guess I'm going
downstairs, then.
Hey.
If you're angry
because of Cleo, just know
I told her to stop being a jerk.
Obviously
she can't tell you where to sit."

With that, Noelle disappears into the hall.

I take the envelope,
stuff it into the bottom of my bag.

I thought it'd be better
for me to hide
and protect myself
so Noelle could never say
she doesn't want to hang out with me.

But if that's true
then why do I feel
so squirmy and wrong inside?

Sharing

I keep all my poems
in the notebook Pop gave me.
The only person
I show them to
is Mrs. V.

After class, she asks
if she can hang one of my poems
up on the classroom board.
"I think the other students
will relate to your poem."

She says it might help
people understand
what's going on in my head.

My poem on the board
would be like
those animal heads
mounted on hunters' walls,

like pulling out my insides
and hanging them up
like Christmas lights.

Besides,
does anyone at Pebblecreek
really want to understand
what's going on in my head?

I shake my head.
I think
I'll keep my poems
safe in my notebook
for now.

Endangered Species

On the way into school, Addie's mom whispers to the
    other moms,
"She needs more discipline. More attention than
    Pebblecreek can offer."
Loud enough for me to hear.

At recess, a teacher pulls me aside
because she thought I was angry
at the girl using the jump rope before me.

Addie no longer sits behind me.
They switched her to the other class.
Her empty seat, a constant reminder.

I go back to my lunch table
but Addie scoots to the far edge away from me,
and Cleo looks at me like she'll catch some disease if she
    sits too close.

At lunch, people whisper that Addie's mom
is threatening to pull Addie and her sisters out
if "violent episodes aren't taken seriously here."

Noelle wrinkles her nose
when Cleo and Gemma give me looks
but doesn't say anything.

What if Mrs. V is wrong?
What if they won't let me stay?
What can I do about it?

I always thought I was part of the Pebblecreek family
but maybe you're only part of the Pebblecreek family
if you're able to be just like everyone else.

Misunderstood

In history, Ms. R keeps me after school.
"I have to ask, Selah, did you do this homework
on your own? Your handwriting changes so much,
it looks like lots of people worked on it."

She shows me the page, where some words
are in blue pen, others in black.
Some letters are in nice clean blocks,
others in faster scribbles. My handwriting
isn't always neat. Sometimes
I get tired or excited
and start writing differently.

"I didn't cheat," I say. "I'd *never*
cheat." Shouldn't Ms. R know that?
Shouldn't everyone at Pebblecreek know
I do my work, that I've always been
a good student? The idea of cheating
makes me so angry, I feel tears
rush up to my eyes.
No one's ever had a problem
with my handwriting before.
Why now?

I know exactly why.

"OK," Ms. R says,
like she doesn't believe me.
"How about I just have
a quick chat with your mom
before you go?"

All the feelings
carbonate inside me
and I try to push them down
but I'm too late.

I ball up on the floor
and cry. I want the old
Pebblecreek. I want things
to go back to how
they used to be, when I
had a place here
and people trusted me. But no matter
how many rules I try to follow
it will never go back.

"Oh, Selah," Ms. R says,
her voice softening.
"Please don't cry."

Good thing the door is closed,
that it's after school,
that no one else can see me like this.

"I haven't taken any points off.
You still have an A on the assignment,"
she says, like that's the point.
Like I care about the grade.

There's so much
people at Pebblecreek
don't understand about me.
If I shared my poems
like Mrs. V suggested,
would they listen?
Would they understand?

Misanthrope

In English class today, we learned the word
"misanthrope":
a person who doesn't like society or people.

Cleo raised her hand and asked,
"So basically Selah?"
and everyone laughed.

Mrs. V sent Cleo to the office,
but it doesn't matter.
Now my new nickname is Misanthrope.

I mean,
it's not *completely* inaccurate.
In class, we read part of *The Misanthrope* (the play)

and I relate to Alcest and how
he's tired of how confusing
and hypocritical
people can be.

Like when he said:

> "Betrayed and wronged in everything,
> I'll flee this bitter world where vice is king,
> and seek some spot unpeopled and apart
> where I'll be free to have an honest heart."

I get that.
How do I find
that place
where I can finally be free
to be honest
and completely
myself?

Mom keeps asking me:

"How are your friends?
I haven't seen
Noelle in a while."
I shrug her off, don't want
to tell her the truth.

Mom says
I should see my friends
but I tell her I'm busy
with homework. That I have to prove
to Pebblecreek
that I'm a Good Student.

I thought she'd be happy
that I'm trying so hard
but instead she sighs
like she's really tired

and heats up some leftover lasagna.

Saturday

Mom pulls out
my birthday tickets to FantasyCon.
She says it's today—
I completely forgot!

I look it up on my computer:
pictures of costumes, panels, art shows
all about fantasy creatures
including dragons.

There's a place like this
that exists?

Mom says Pop found it online.
There are two tickets,
so I assume she'll drop us off
and it'll be
me and Pop.

It's only when we're in the car
and Mom drives past Pop's,
goes the way she does
when picking me up after school,
that I realize it means
me and Noelle.

Noelle and I

don't say much on the drive there.
Mom keeps asking Noelle
about school
and Noelle answers
the way everyone answers parents:
short, right answers,
tight,
with no room for asking
much more.

Noelle plays with the end
of her ponytail,
keeps looking at me
with her eyebrows arched,
lips scrunched,
like she can't believe
she has to be stuck here
all day
with a school criminal.

I scoot in my seat
closest to the window
to give her max space
away from a weirdo like me.

FantasyCon

As soon as the door opens, I know
this is my favorite place in the world.

In the lobby, people are dressed up
like unicorns, elves, fairies, and dragons,
carrying foam swords
and posing for pictures.

I wish I had a costume.
All I have is my poem-notebook,
and a T-shirt with Toothless
from *How to Train Your Dragon*.

Even Noelle can't stop
her eyes from darting around
the artist tables
the costume contest
the different panel rooms
people walk in and out of.

Noelle points to a line of wizards
wearing real and fake beards
and purple and blue robes
and wands and hats
and says,
"Dude. If only I'd known
to bring *my* wizard outfit!"

And she laughs
while my mind digs
through her closet and bedroom.
"What wizard outfit?"
I ask,

and she elbows me
like her elbow
is the hilt of a sword.

"That's the joke,"
she says,

and I laugh,
because that's what you're supposed to do
when people tell jokes.

Walking through the Artist Alley,

I get four compliments
on my Toothless shirt.
"That's my favorite movie series,"
at least two artists say
behind their booths.

I grin.
How many people at Pebblecreek
have actually seen, let alone love
How to Train Your Dragon
like I do?

There are so many things
with dragons on them:
pouches, pencil cases, skirts,
posters, jewelry—even
hand-stitched plushes.
I want to buy everything.
Even Noelle keeps stopping
to admire
the *Lord of the Rings* fan art,
a Legolas costume,
a leather notebook that says "There and Back Again,"
even a *Lord of the Rings* handmade chess set.

"This is a magical, wonderful place,"
Noelle says,
and I grin and nod
and wonder
if maybe
not everything
is broken
between us.

Pouring In

I stop
at a stand
where a person sells
dragon necklaces
dragon ear cuffs
shoulder dragons
dragons you can wear on your arm.

"You can try one on,"
they say.
"The silicone is smooth
and has this great weight to it.
Having it on calms me down
when I get overstimulated."

Their T-shirt says:
"Just be yourself,
but if you can be a dragon,
then just be a dragon."

I slide a bright red dragon
around my arm
and understand what they mean.
The weight on my arm
is calming, the smooth texture
cooling like water.

"Overstimulated?" I ask.
A new word to me.

The dragon seller tucks
a loose strand of black hair
behind their ear.
"Like when everything feels
like it's pouring in
and there's no room
for all the feelings to go.

You know?"

I nod so hard
I feel like my head will fall off.
I *absolutely* know.

Open Mic

We look at our schedules
and outline an afternoon
of screenings, panels, and concerts.

At the bottom of the schedule,
a square catches my eye:
an all-day open mic.

POETRY!

it screams
from the page.

Mrs. V's voice
echoes in my head,
telling me to share my poems,

but I push it down.
Would they even like my poem?
Or would they think I'm a freak,

like everyone at Pebblecreek does?
Being here, I've felt light
like a bubble, not worrying

about school, free
of that anxious current in my chest.
I'm having *fun*—why ruin that?

I don't mark the event,
but I don't need to. Throughout the day,
no matter what I do,

it pulses through my head:
Open mic. All day.
Cecil Ballroom.

Too Much of a Good Thing

All the conversations around us
and the loud, excited voices
and bumping into people
and waiting in line
and the ten songs playing from different rooms
are churning inside me.

I feel my inner dragon
throbbing,
wanting to break out and scream.

Part of me wants
to find a quiet place
away from all the noise
and hide
until I can recharge,

but the rest of me
wants to be *here*,
in the middle of it all,
taking everything in.

Mrs. V says I should
communicate,
but what would I say?
It's not like I want to leave.
I don't want to miss
a minute of anything.

So I guess I have to
push through
like usual
like the rules say
until we get home.

No More Room

When we sit down for the concert,
the seats are hard. My legs ache
from all the standing and walking.
My head gets fuzzy, like my body thinks
because I'm sitting down it's time to go to bed.

Noelle leans over to me, her voice low:
"Selah, are you alright?"

Is it obvious?
I look down at my fingers, squeezing.
My muscles, clenching.
Tapping my teeth
to the beat of the music
playing from the speakers
before the concert begins.

Her eyebrows furrow.
"I don't know why
you've been ignoring me
since the whole thing with Addie,
but it's not like I can't see
that something's wrong."

Of course.
After Addie,
everyone thinks there's something
wrong with me.
Even Noelle.

I mean,
I *knew* that,
but to hear it
makes my whole head sting.

I want to tell her
I know she doesn't want to be here

with me right now.
I know I'm not Normal.
I know I can never *be* the Normal
she wants me to be,

but then the band gets onstage
dressed in corsets and dragon wings.

Colored lights flash across the stage
like a sped-up thunderstorm.
A guitar screams through the speakers,
then the crackly crumbs of a piano,
and the main singer's voice
scratching like sandpaper
against my ear's wall.

Everyone's screams and cheers
charge into me like an army
pushing
until there's no more room
left inside me.

I get up from my seat
and run.

Air

As if underwater,
frantically flailing
for the surface,

my body knows
I can only survive so long
in this loud, crowded hallway.

I push through lines,
eyes wide,
looking for the bathrooms.

When I find them,
there's a line, and people
complain as I push past them,

past the girl in the front of the line
into the one open
swinging stall door.

Then I can
finally

breathe.

Earplugs

There's something safe
about hiding behind a stall door.
Even though I know
everyone in the bathroom
can see my gray-brown sneakers
and hear me crying,
it's like I'm covered in a force field,
like when you're a kid at recess,
playing tag
with your feet on the blacktop safe zone,
untaggable.

I pull out my poem-notebook,
try to find words for the feelings,
trying to breathe so
I can go back out
and Noelle
won't be mad.

Then I hear
a knock on my stall door.
Is someone going
to yell at me,
make me get out?

"Hey, I think I just saw you
coming from the concert?"
they ask.
"A bit of a sensory
overload in there, isn't it?"

That voice is familiar—
the dragon seller?

They slide a baggie
of two orange earplugs
across the bathroom tile.

"I always keep extras with me
at cons like this. Lots of us
use sensory tools here—
sometimes I'll wear them
the whole day!"

I open the bag,
pinch the orange foam
between my fingers,
and shove them
one by one
into my ears,

then everything around me
slowly crinkles away
as the foam expands,
padding me in an envelope
away from the rest of the world

like *magic*.

Outside the bathroom,

Noelle stands, her eyes wide,
eyebrows creased. Angled. Voice
loud, even through the earplugs.
"What happened?" she asks.
"You just disappeared
and I was *freaking* out."

I look for words.
"I was feeling . . .
bad. The dragon seller called it
overstimulation.
But they gave me
earplugs and I feel
a lot better now."

Noelle nods
but doesn't smile,
her eyes asking
a million questions.

"They said
lots of people
use stuff like this here,"
I say. "They called it
sensory tools?"

"Just please don't disappear again,
OK? Your mom
would kill us."
Noelle finally smiles.
"Good thing I've known you
long enough to guess
you were probably
hiding in the bathroom."

We look at each other
and it's almost Normal again:

me and **Noelle**
like we were before,

but then she buries her head
in our marked-up schedule.

"So. No more concerts.
They weren't that good
anyway.
How about we go back
to the Artist Alley?
It's not as loud out there."

I nod.
Maybe Noelle
doesn't completely hate me
after all
but it's too soon
to know for sure.

Like a Dragon

I walk around
with earplugs in my ears
and feel
briefly
invincible.

Bracelets

In the hallway
there's a table
covered in rubber bracelets.

Sets of three:
red, green, yellow
like a traffic light.

The woman at the table
wearing an R2-D2 shirt
tells me they're free,

that I can wear these
to tell people around me
how much I want to interact.

Green means *I'm doing fine!*
Yellow, *I need space.*
Red, *Please don't talk to me.*

Around the woman's wrist,
a green bracelet.
"As someone on the spectrum,

I can go from green to red
pretty quickly,
and my husband says

he's still getting used to
the signs of when
I need to be left alone."

"The spectrum?" I ask.

"The autism spectrum."
She smiles. Her eyes
fix on my ears.

"Good idea with those earplugs."
She pats her pocket.
"I have mine in here too."

Lots of questions
bubble up inside me
like carbonation, but I grab

a set of bracelets
and put on the yellow one.
Just a half hour ago,

I would've been red.
Now yellow. Maybe,
with enough time,
I'll be green again.

Wearable Words

"Do you want some?" I ask Noelle,
playing with the bracelet on my wrist.

She shakes her head.
"If I need someone to leave me alone,
I'll just tell them to leave me alone."

The woman laughs.
"I always think I'm going to do that
but then, when I need to,
I can't find the words!
So the bracelets help me
when words can't."

Noelle nods, studies me,
grabs a set of bracelets,
and stuffs them in her pocket.

Helping

Walking through the Artist Alley,
we keep passing back and forth
in front of the door
to Cecil Ballroom.

Even with my earplugs,
I can hear the applause,
the little bits of poems.

In my bag, I feel
my poem-notebook
heavy like an anchor.

I've never wanted
to share my poems before,
but inside my chest,
I feel my heart jump
on my stomach's trampoline
no matter how hard
I try to ignore it.

I *want* the words out.
I *want* to stop holding them in.

The dragon seller.
The bracelet woman.
They *helped* me.
Maybe sharing my poems here
can help too.

"Let's check this out,"
I tell Noelle
and walk into Cecil Ballroom.

Sign-Up

Inside Cecil Ballroom
is *quiet.*
Like the road
in front of our house
in the middle of the night.
Like Pebblecreek over summer break.

A girl with pink hair
walks up to a makeshift stage,
pulls out a sheet of paper,
and reads.

The room is filled
with mostly teens and adults,
silent in their seats,
listening,
until she finishes

and they
explode
in cheers.

On the edge of the row,
the dragon seller
waves at me.

I grin back and mouth,
Thank you, pointing to
the earplugs in my ears.

A boy with a nose ring
sitting by the door
holds a clipboard up to us.
"Want to sign up?"
he asks.

Noelle looks at me.
"What is this?" she asks,

but the boy answers for me.
"It's an open mic!
You can share
anything you'd like."

Noelle laughs,
fingers tucking her light brown hair
behind her ear
like she always does
before debate presentations.

As I grab the clipboard
and write down my name,
she frowns.
"What are you going
to share?
One of your pictures?"

I shake my head.
"Something else."

We sit down,
Noelle shuffling in her seat
until they call for
Selah Godfrey.

I go up to the mic,
pull out my poem-notebook,
close my eyes, pretend
I'm in the perfect dark,
and start reading:

Selah the "Weird Girl"

By Selah Godfrey

I know I'm the weird girl.
I don't like to look you in the eye.

I wish I could wear a sign that says:
"Please Don't Touch Me."

Hugs from strangers burn like blacktop
on a sunny day. Every word

through every wall sticks to my ears
like bugs to sticky flypaper.

Sometimes I don't feel like talking.
Sometimes there are no words left in my mouth.

I don't brush my hair unless Mom makes me—
it's a waste of time and I can feel every hair pull on my scalp.

I'll forget to text you back because
I only use my phone in emergencies,

and I don't have any social media profiles.
I don't care about what songs everyone else listens to.

All I care about are dragons
and drawing dragons and writing poems

because dragons don't care if you think
they're weird or not. Dragons fly

wherever they want to go; no one
can stop them. And poems

make me feel like a dragon.

After my reading,

people come up to me,
say things like:

Your piece was my favorite

Are you sure we aren't

the same person?

I feel that way too, but you put it into words so well.

There was so much feeling.

Are you on the spectrum too?

I think everyone in my social skills group would love *your poem.*

You should publish that poem.

I thought it was just me.

Noelle says:
I didn't know
you wrote poems.

That night

I can't sleep.
My battery is charged so full.

I still feel
the thrill of sharing onstage
of everyone's smiles
of being fully myself
of how they *got it*
buzzing through my body.

The dragon inside me
opens its wings
and wants to fly
out over the front yard.
I flap my hands
like *I* might fly away too.

I clap my hands
click my teeth
bury my face in my pillow
which feels like
the softest pillow in the world.

I can hear
the night wind
miles away
blow through our woods.
I can hear it so clear
it's like I'm out there
like I'm everywhere at once.

I feel so
alive
and electric, bursting
like the whole world
is having a dance party inside me
and I'm dancing along with it.

It's a
BIG
feeling,
but a
GOOD
one.

Before tonight,
I thought feeling only meant:
something hurting
someone saying it shouldn't hurt
something tucked away deep in my chest
shame

But right now
I realize this:

I am
so
fully
here
in every moment.

I am so
alive,

a beating heart
connected
to the whole world
around me.

I might not be able
to fly or breathe
fire
but I can write
poems
that people get
which is maybe
the best power of all.

I get out of bed.
I jump up and down
and get the jumps out of me.
I pull out my poem-notebook
from my backpack
and write and write
until I can calm down enough
to fall asleep.

New Words

On Monday,
all day at school,
new words
buzz through my head
from FantasyCon.

When I get home,
I get on my computer
and search:

overstimulated
autism spectrum
sensory tools

I read until Mom calls me for dinner.
I read when I should be sleeping.
I print out more things to read at school between classes.

Autism is a word
I've heard before
but it's never been said
like it's a good thing.

People say "autism"
the same way
they say things like
"cancer."

But the more I read,
the more I realize
autism can be
and look like
lots of things.
That's why it's called
a spectrum.

Autistic people struggle
with things like

communication
change
social interactions.

They love
repetition
routines
special interests.

Everything I read says
that's ME!

Maybe that's why
noises and lights sting
words are hard to find
I like rules
and why
I feel like a dragon.

I never would've thought I was,
but before FantasyCon,
before reading,
I had no idea what autism is.

A brand-new world
opens up
through my screen.

I take notes
save links
feel poems burst inside my chest
like fireworks.

I am full
of possibilities—

I can do more
than just hide.

Things I Like about Me

I love the texture of oil pastels
between my fingers,
the satisfaction of drawing
a perfect curve,
the cozy feeling
in drawing eye after eye.

I love the even back and forth
of swinging on my swing set
and the way it lets my mind fly.
I love how the oily smell of Pop's basement
makes my brain smile, how talking with Pop
about trains and myths
and how to build an engine from scratch
charges me with energy.

I love the familiar sound
of the *Lord of the Rings* soundtrack
every time Noelle and I
watch the movies together at her house,
and the calming sound
of Mrs. V's voice
in the oasis of English class.

Sometimes I click my teeth
even though my dentist says I shouldn't
because my jaw likes to move
to the rhythm of songs
and chew on ice.

Sometimes I blink real hard
or squeeze my hands into fists
or scribble in my notebook
when the feelings inside me
are too big for words. I love the way
feelings pump through
my whole body like blood,

how alive I am
from everything I feel.

Sometimes I jump
because
sometimes you've just gotta jump.

Secret Weapon

I wake up,
look out my windows
and see the neighbors
starting a bonfire.

Inside my chest
I can feel my heart
panic, preparing
for the loud to come.

I go over to my backpack,
reach into the pockets,
crawl my fingers over
crumbled granola bar crumbs,
ripped bits of paper,
broken pencil lead,
and find my orange earplugs.

I twist one into my left ear
another into my right
and feel the foam
expand, like a blanket
surrounding my thoughts,

and I don't wake up again
until my alarm goes off
in the morning.

Not Ready

I tell Mrs. V I'm ready
and she shows me
the bulletin board
where I can hang my poem.

Mrs. V said
if I didn't want to read it out loud
this would be a way for everyone
to still enjoy my poem
and hear my voice. Maybe
if they hear my voice,
people will understand
why I am the way I am
and Principal Merkert
won't kick me out.

I pin up the poem
and walk out
to Mom's van
but on the drive home
my muscles tense
my thoughts loop
doubt fizzes through me like soda.

At night I think about
all the bad things
people might say about my poem.
How they might not understand
my "normal-person mask,"
or why I feel like a dragon.
Even without my name on it,
they'll recognize my dragon drawing.
What if they make fun of me?
What if I get in trouble
and this is the "problem"
that gets me kicked out?

In the morning, I convince Mom
to bring me to school early.
I run through the halls
(even though Mrs. Tucker tells me
to stop running)
to the bulletin board
rip my poem down
stuff it in my folder
hope no one saw it

and try to not think about
the tear I made in the process
cutting through my drawn dragon's neck.

Wordless

As soon as I took my poem down,
my words went with it.
All day in class, I hope
no one will call on me
because my words are missing.
My mouth is locked.
I pull out my red wristband
but what's the point?
No one listens to my wristbands
the same way they wouldn't listen
to my poems.

Ezra notices.
"Quiet today.
Plotting who'll be
your next victim? It's always
the quiet ones."

He watches me,
like he wants me to hit him.

I want to crawl under my desk
and into the floor.

Wish List

At home, I escape
into my computer.

Online I find a whole shop
of tools for people like me:

chewelry
fidget spinners
bubble pops
thinking putty
Koosh balls
weighted plushes
communication bracelets,
     like the ones we got at FantasyCon

I send Mom the link and ask her
for one of everything for Christmas.

Mom scrolls through the store,
a confused look on her face.
"Sweetie, aren't you a little
old
for these kinds of toys?"

"They aren't toys," I say.
"They're tools. To help me
at Pebblecreek."

Mom strokes my hair
and grabs her car keys.
"Sweetie, you are doing
great. I don't think you need
things like this."

My chest deflates
like a week-old balloon.
How do I make Mom understand?

Good Different

Later that day,
when we get in the car,
I decide to tell Mom
about the dragon inside me:

"Mom,
it's not just Pop
or the dentist
or Principal Merkert
who think I'm different.
My teacher thinks so too."

Mom frowns.
"Sweetie,
people think
all kinds of things
but don't let it
discourage you.
There's
nothing
wrong with you."

But there *is*
something. Not
wrong, but *there*.

Saying there's nothing
just makes me feel worse,
like I'm melting
through the car seat
and becoming
an invisible ghost.

No, it's OK,
I want to say. It's a
good
kind of different.

But the words
stay stuck in my throat.

Mom,
why
do we have to
care
so much
about Normal?

No More Meltdowns

If Mom won't order me
sensory tools,
I'll have to make my own.

I come to school
prepared
like a dragon into battle:

gummies
to chew
and keep my mouth happy

sunglasses
for the bright fluorescent lights

earplugs
for the loud hallways

a stress ball
to keep my hands happy

and my notebook and pencils
obviously.

I feel safe
with my sunglasses on,
protected
by my earplugs,
like I'm walking inside
a clear force field.

A couple kids look at me funny in the halls.
"Why are you wearing sunglasses inside?" Ezra laughs.
But I keep going on my way.

I realize
I don't really care what Ezra thinks.

In homeroom,

Mr. S doesn't like my tools.
He stops talking when I start chewing my gummies.
"No eating in class, SELL-uh. You know that."

"It's not eating," I say. How do I explain
how my insides dance
and my brain sparks
when I'm chewing on something?

Mr. S frowns. "Are you being smart with me?"

I don't understand what he means.
"Some people say I'm smart," I say.

The room fills with giggles and gasps.
I definitely didn't understand what he meant.

Mr. S comes over and pulls the sunglasses off my head.
"Do you want to be sent to the office?"

I shake my head,
No, no, no!
I don't need
one more strike
against me.

He puts my sunglasses on his head,
holds his hand out open.
"Then I need your contraband."
My earplugs, gummies, stress ball,
all laid out in his palm.
Why
are things that help me
against the rules?

He takes my tools,
puts them in a drawer in his desk,
and keeps talking,

my sunglasses still on his head
like my pain is just
another one of his jokes.

I bite my lip,
keep my eyes on my desk
and my pencil taking notes.
Don't cry. Don't
scream. Not here,
not where Mr. S can think
he's won.

Of Course

Of course I told Pop about what Mr. S did.
Not Mom though. Mom would probably side
with Mr. S and say he had every right
to take my tools. But the next morning,

when Ezra looks out the window between class
and calls out, "Who's that old man?"
and everyone crowds to the window,
I don't expect to see Pop, storming into Pebblecreek,
his orange sunglasses on his head.

"He looks like he's gonna beat someone up!" Ezra yells
and everyone won't stop talking.

I ask Mr. S if I can go to the bathroom
but sprint down the stairs instead.

Even from the stairwell
I can hear Pop's not-inside-voice:
"Suspending her . . . now stealing from her?
How do you expect my daughter
to keep paying through the nose
when you bozos keep bullying
my granddaughter?"

I stiffen. No one's allowed
to talk at Pebblecreek like that.
Mrs. Tucker tries to speak
in her calming voice
but Pop will not be calmed.

The front doors open and Mom bursts in,
her head a half-brushed cloud of hairspray and hair,
no makeup.
She's become really good at finding Pop
even when
he probably doesn't want her to find him.

She runs by so fast,
like she didn't even see me,
her voice joining Pop's
in a who-can-be-the-loudest competition:

"What are you *doing*? You think this is *helping*?
Do you ever
think
how what you do
impacts Selah? Or me?
They said one more problem
and Selah's gone. Thanks to you,
it could all be over now."

One more problem. That's what
I am to people now, even
my mom. A
problem.

I've heard enough. It feels
wrong,
listening to them argue.
My breaths get faster fasterfasterfaster.
I run back up the stairs
to the bathroom,
hide in a stall,

breathe   in
breathe   out

until I calm down enough
to go back to class.

At the end of the day,

Mr. S gives me
a ziplock bag with my tools inside.

"You know now
to keep these at home,
right?" he asks,
and I nod, even though
I've read online
that plenty of schools
let kids have the tools they need.
Inside I scream,
You just want to keep
me
at home.

Outside
kids huddle by the parking lot
in sweaters and coats.
Through their whispers
I hear them gossip:

   Selah's grandad totally beat up Principal Merkert

  so angry . . . so scary

     those weirdo Godfreys

crazy must run in the family.

Pop Goes Missing

The house is quiet.
Since we got home from school,
Mom's heels have been tapping

across the floor, but now
it's late and Mom
is probably in bed.

From my window
I see something move.
The neighbors?

My heart does jumping
jacks in my chest.
I leave my blank page

on my desk
and get up to find
Mom, in the dark

with her pink robe,
slippers,
and a flashlight

calling for Pop
in the wet road
like he's a missing dog.

I open the front door
and a burst of cold air
rushes in,

but when Mom sees me,
she tells me to go back inside.

"I got cross at him,"
Mom says.
I know. I heard.

She bites her lip.
Red lipstick smears
the edge of her tooth.

"He's not answering
his phone
and his bike's been gone
for a while. I don't know
where he is."

"Maybe he's just taking
one of his walks," I say,
but Mom doesn't look convinced.

I can't tell
if it's rain or tears
making Mom's face wet.

She doesn't say anything,
but turns back to the road,
calling, "Dad, Dad.

Please come home."

Favorite Spot

Mom is too busy
in the road,
so I cut through the woods
behind her.

I check all of Pop's favorite spots:
the cul-de-sac at the end of our street
the clearing where new houses are being built
the trail we made through the woods
between our two houses.

He can't be far.
Why is Mom so worried?
Pop likes to go on walks
but he always comes back. He's always
fine. He's Pop after all.

Powerless

In the woods behind his house,
I find Pop,
mud-caked slippers on his feet.

He's standing by
some trees
wrapped in orange strings.

He sees me coming
through the rain
and says,

"Your mother just doesn't get us,
does she? I don't know
why she keeps you in that
hoity-toity school."

I *like* Pebblecreek,
I almost say,
but with how things are now,
is it still true?

"Can we go inside?"
I ask,
peeling my wet hair
away from my eyes.

Pop nods
and we walk through the woods
to his house.

I pull out my phone
and text Mom
that Pop's safe.

Pop's House

We go into the kitchen
and I realize I haven't been up here
or anywhere but his workshop
since Grammy died.

The kitchen table is covered
with pages of typewritten poems
and newspapers
from weeks ago.

An avalanche
of stacked old books
on the B&O Railroad
melt onto the floor.

Pop has to rearrange
the stuff on the kitchen counter
like a puzzle
to find the tea.

The living room
has stacks of empty boxes
from his online buys,
and the dust on the TV cabinet

is thick like icing.
The candy bowl, empty.
My body goes stiff,
being in such a full space.

"Your mom keeps trying
to move all my things around,"
he says. "I'm a grown man,
for Pete's sake. I don't need
someone coming in to keep up my house.
It's fine the way it is."

I don't know about that.
I usually side with Pop
but maybe this is something
where Mom is right
and Pop is wrong.

Talking to Pop over Tea

Mom was really scared
when she didn't know
where you were

> Oh, your mother
> always takes everything
> so seriously
> even more so
> after everything with your father

She seemed really upset

> Your mother's
> bottled everything up
> since she was a little girl

> She's never understood
> that I can't do that

> That it's just how I feel
> in that moment

But you *know* it upsets her

> She should know by now
> to not get so upset

> I always come back

> Everyone needs
> some alone time now and then

> It's just
> how
> I am

Maybe

Maybe my rules
worry too much about
what other people think

Maybe Pop's rules
don't think enough
about how other people feel

Words

Mom comes through the door,
the rain screaming behind her
like someone's pulling
the sky by its hair.

Mom's dripping wet,
her once-pink robe
now mud brown.

She looks so small
in the doorway,
smaller than me.

"Daddy,"
she says.

There are so many
more words in her—
I can see them in her eyes,
bouncing to get out,

but she bites her lip.

"Sue, you gotta stop
worrying so much,"
Pop says.

Words surge through my chest
like a geyser
and I don't want to risk
keeping them down
and losing them.

"Pop,
maybe instead
you should stop doing things
that make her worry."

A Good Point

The biggest rule of all
broken:
Don't say anything
that might sound
rude.

"Selah,"
Mom snaps,
but she doesn't move,
her body stiff
like a telephone pole.

Pop doesn't say anything
at first, his expression
flickering like a candle
between
annoyance and laughing.

Finally, he smiles,
digs his hands in his pockets
and says,
"Well, kiddo,
maybe you've got
a good point there."

Not the Only One

Mom and I
walk through the dark wet grass
back home.

The frogs burp,
the crickets chirp,
a car drives somewhere in the distance.

But besides that, silence.

"I don't like how you talked to Pop,"
Mom says,
"but thank you
for sticking up for me."

Her hand
rubs a whirlpool
light against my back.

It's Mom's hand:
too familiar, too thoughtful
to burn.

The only thing
that burns
is the thought

that maybe I'm not
the only one
stuffing things inside,

that there are words
still stuck in Mom,
unspoken.

Poem for Pop

Pop,

You always tell me
that feelings are like
steam inside us
and steam is hot
but it doesn't just burn us.
It can burn other people around us too.

You always tell me
to write poems
about my feelings
so maybe you should write
a poem to Mom.

But also
you probably should let Mom
help you clean up the house.
It's pretty messy in there.

Sharing

I carefully rip
the page out of my notebook
along the seam of the binding,

fold it up,

and stick it in Pop's mailbox.

Party

Noelle's party is today.
Her invite still sits
at the bottom of my backpack.

FantasyCon was fun.
We were almost
Normal again,

but now we're back
in the real world
where I have no idea
what she's thinking or feeling.

It's not too late
to tell Mom. We could still
get there in time. Maybe
I'd actually have fun.

But even if the girls
don't give me weird stares,
even if I bring
my earplugs and sunglasses,
the noise and lights
and all the people in one room
might be too much.
Is it worth it?

Maybe Noelle's mom didn't make her invite me.
Maybe Noelle really does want to stay friends.
Or maybe she doesn't.

I don't tell Mom about the party.
Instead I get my notebook,
open to a blank page
for a poem for Noelle.

I should write something to her

like I did to Pop
but what? I try to find
words in my notebook,
but nothing comes out.

Evening

Everyone's probably
having lots of fun
at Noelle's party right now.

As I dig in my backpack for pencils,
the unicorn key chain Noelle gave me
catches my eye.

Pop isn't always fair
in what he does with his feelings.
Have I been unfair to Noelle too?

I still have
no idea
how to talk to Noelle,

but maybe I don't
need to know.
I just need to get up

the way I did
to share my poem:
open up my chest to show

what's going on inside me
and wait
and see what happens.

If she's my friend
she'll still like me
how I am, as is.

If she hates me,
it's not like things
can get any worse.

Sunday Morning

When Noelle opens the front door,
she tries to smile
but I see her eyebrows hopping up
like crickets.
She doesn't want me here.

"My birthday party was yesterday, you know,"
she says, her lips pulled
into a smirk—a friendly joke?
Or is she making fun of me?

This was a mistake.

I thought
maybe
after sharing my poems
I could do anything
maybe even
convince Noelle
we could be friends again.

But I've waited too long.

Mom's still in the driveway.
If I run, I can go back to the car
and never bother Noelle again.

When I turn away,
Noelle calls after me.

FantasyCon must've been an exception.

But then I feel
her hand on my shoulder,
a thousand little prickle-shocks
like an electric cactus
ripple through my skin.

"Why are you being
so weird?"
she asks.

I wait for her to bring up
hiding in the bathroom at sleepovers
refusing to dive in the pool
hitting Addie
disappearing at FantasyCon
what a weird, annoying friend I've been.
My muscles clench,
waiting for her anger.

But she sighs.
"I thought we were friends
but you haven't told me *anything*.
You're ignoring me at school.
And that poem you read—
what's *really* going on?"

Me, ignoring her?
I thought she was ignoring *me*.
I thought she didn't want me
to bother her
with my not-Normal-ness,
that she'd rather me
stay in my cave.
There's nothing more rude
than forcing someone
to be friends with you.

I open my mouth
but can't find the words.
I should've just written
a poem for Noelle
and shoved it in her mailbox.

Eventually, I find:
"I don't know.
I'm sorry.

I know I'm a total
weirdo
and I get it if you don't want to be
friends with me anymore."

Noelle stares at me.
A silver SUV drives around
the cul-de-sac of silence
between us.

She says,
"Sure,
you're weird
but so am I
and why would I not
want to be friends anymore?
Why would you even think that?"

I take in a breath.
Why *did* I think that—
because of the rules?

"You're not weird," I say.

Noelle laughs.
"Weird's a weird word."

Then we go inside
and make microwaved nachos
and stuff our mouths
with gooey cheese.

Why

Once we've peeled
all the microwaved cheese
off the plate,
Noelle gets quiet.
Her eyes focus
out the window,
into the pool.

"Why didn't you tell me
what was going on?
I don't even know
why you thought
I was angry at you."

I fumble for words
but can't find any.

"It has to do with Addie,
right?"

I play with
my green wristband,
wish it was yellow.

"You didn't get it,"
I finally manage.
"Why I hit Addie.
I'd been trying
so hard
to keep those things
inside me,
but Addie made them all
tumble out."

Noelle doesn't say anything for a minute.
She shrugs.
"Yeah, I mean,

I don't get
you sometimes.
But so what?
Did you really think
I wouldn't wanna be friends
over something like that?"

Even if

I had all the words in the world,
I wouldn't have
any words
for that.

How many times
have I been angry
because people assumed
things about me—

yet this whole time,
how much have I assumed
about Noelle?
About
everyone
else?

The Only Words I Can Find:

"I'm sorry."

Back

Noelle nods
but doesn't smile.
Her eyes
focus on the counter.

My rules used to say
that if you say "I'm sorry"
you'll know the other person
won't stay angry at you
anymore, and things
can go back to Normal.

But it's obvious
right now
how silly
how babyish
that rule was.

Noelle's finger
traces the counter.
"No. *I'm* sorry.
I didn't know what to do.
I still don't know
what to do; I just want
to be friends again.
I don't understand
all the stuff
you're going through
but you can tell me, OK?
I might not be a fast learner
but I still want
to learn."

I nod
and nod
until it feels like

my head might fall off.
"Me too. More
than anything
in the world."

Colored Feelings

1.

I've started wearing my bracelets
everywhere.
In the morning, I'm usually
green,
and as the day goes on,
I reach for the yellow in my pocket.
Between classes, I play with
red
but don't always
have to put it on.

Earlier this week,
in line for PE,
Noelle saw my fingers
pulling at the red band
and told Mr. Cochrain,
"Selah's not been feeling
very good today
and probably should rest—
is that right, Selah?"
I smiled and nodded.
Good thing Noelle
has enough words
for the two of us.

2.

"Why do you keep
switching your bracelets?"
Ezra asked yesterday morning.
I had them laid out on my desk.
"Can't make up your mind?
Green, red, yellow. What are you,
a traffic light?"

Sort of, I wanted to say
but couldn't find the words.
As if Ezra would've listened.

My new nickname now
is Traffic Light
and every time I walk past
in the hall
the boys like to make
loud siren sounds,
which doesn't even make sense,
but it's not like Ezra ever makes sense.

Today
Noelle has started
wearing her bracelets too—
mostly green,
but every now and then
I catch a glimpse of yellow
in the halls.

Ready

In history class,
we talked about
Martin Luther,
who had a problem
with the church
and said something about it
by hanging up
ninety-five arguments on the door
for everyone to see.

I couldn't help but think about
my poems
and how maybe
hanging my poems
would not just help me
get out my feelings
but help change things for the better.

After school,
I knock on
Mrs. V's office door.

I tell her
I'm ready to share
my poems.

Everywhere

After school,
when all the students have filed outside
and only the teachers are left
grading at their desks,

Mrs. V's printer
keeps running out of paper,
printing out my poems.

They don't have my name on them,
but I know they're mine
and that's what matters to me.

Mrs. V and I
talked about different ways
we could share my poems,

but I wanted something
you could reach out and feel
with your hands,
something you'd have to see
everywhere you go,
something you couldn't run away from.

All the bulletin boards

in Pebblecreek's halls
have one or more
of my poems.

We had to use
every pushpin
in Mrs. V's desk
to get them up,

but seeing my words
loud
and un-ignorable
is one of the biggest feelings
I've ever felt:

like I could break out flying
in the middle of the hall
while also throwing up my lunch.

Pebblecreek Family

Do you know my name?
I thought families knew each other's names,
but you forget, or say it wrong,
or give me a mean nickname instead.

I hear the things you say about me.
The not-really-compliments you think I'll miss.
I see how you look at me,
that you don't trust me
even though we've known each other for so long.

I don't think your jokes are funny.
I don't like that kids that mess up are called crazy
while bullies are "normal" and fine.
I don't like that instead of helping me,
you think I'm "a problem"
and take away my tools,
that you want me in the office
instead of my classroom.

I always liked that at Pebblecreek
we always say: "You are loved
and worthy and can do great things."

It shouldn't be something
we just say, but something
we do. Everyone here should feel
loved and worthy. Everyone here
can do great things.

In the morning

as classrooms fill up
to start the day,
I watch people
through the crack in the door
stopping in the hall,
reading my poems.

I clench my teeth
and legs
and the smuggled stress ball in my pocket,
watching,
waiting for a response.

What if everyone laughs?
What if people crumple them up
and throw them in trash balls
across the hallway?

Kids come into the seventh-grade class
and take their seats,
whispering things like:

Did you see those poems?
Yeah—weird, right?
They were really good!
Sometimes I feel that way too.
It was like they read my mind.
I didn't know other people felt different here too . . .
Is that one about Mr. S?
He is always threatening to send people to the office . . .
And his jokes aren't funny either!
Who wrote them?
I don't get it—why are these poems there?
You think they'll get in trouble?
Can you even say stuff like that about school?
So what? Putting those out for everyone to read?
    Respect.

In the hallway,

I catch a glimpse
of Principal Merkert
talking to Mrs. V,
one of my poems
in his hand.

Mrs. V
takes it from him,
walks away
in her purple high heels,
and pins it back up
on the board.

Even after Nightmares, You Wake Up

Coming back from lunch,
I see red Sharpie marks
biting the edges
of my poems:

WEIRDO
CRAZY
LOL

Each word
is a bolt of lightning
shooting through me,
rooting me in place.

The dragon inside me
wakes up,
pacing through my chest.

Part of me wants
to run to the bathroom
lock myself in a stall
and cry,

but another part
wants to write more poems
print more poems
until there are so many
the mean words can't keep up.

Like Nothing Happened

The next day,
all of my poems
are gone.

Problem

In the middle of class,
Principal Merkert comes to the door
and asks if I can see him in his office.

I feel
the whole room's ooooooohs
build up like pressure in a volcano
but everyone keeps their lips
tightly pressed
and silent.

My heart erupts.
What did I do
wrong
this time?

I've been writing poems.
I've been wearing my bracelets.
I've even been making a "concerted effort" to smile
and prove to everyone
that even though I'm different
I'm not some dangerous bomb
that will go off
if you look at me funny.

But no one goes
to Principal Merkert's office
for good things,

and as we walk,
he says nothing,
his loud steps echoing
down the hall,

and I'm sure I've definitely
done something
wrong.

Consider

In Principal Merkert's office,
Mom is already sitting
against the wall,
wearing a Polite smile,
even though
her pink-painted fingernails
pick at the eczema
on her thumb.

When Principal Merkert sits down,
he folds his hands,
focuses
his eyes on the desk,
and lets out a sigh.

"Ms. Godfrey,
It's come to my attention
that Selah has been posting
poems throughout the school.
Poems criticizing Pebblecreek."

I frown.
Criticizing?
Is that all he sees?
Mrs. V let me hang up those poems,
I want to say,
but the words
won't come out of my mouth.

Mom's smile
is gone.
"Poems?
Are you telling me

my daughter is in trouble
for writing poems?"

Principal Merkert
pulls at the hairs
on his beard.

"The poems are disruptive.
They're clearly about
someone at Pebblecreek,
and they complain about the school.
I've spoken to her teacher, and—"

"So her teacher knows about the poems?
Then why isn't she here to speak on them?"
Mom's voice shakes.

"This isn't just about
the poems, Ms. Godfrey.
Some of the parents and staff
have expressed concerns
about Selah's . . .
unpredictable
behavior, and of course,
the suspension
earlier this year.

All this to say, we'd like you
to consider
a different school
for Selah in the fall.
We think
Pebblecreek Academy
may not be
the best fit
for Selah's needs."

Any sense
of Mom's usual calm
is quickly
evaporating.
Her body shakes
like an earthquake,
her voice rising
like a volcano.
"Unpredictable?
Because she lost control
once?"

                    Principal Merkert fidgets in his seat.

"This goes against
what you said at our last meeting.
You can't dismiss Selah
because of one *mistake.*
We all make
mistakes.
Surely Selah's not
the only student
who's made a mistake here."

                    "I understand that, Ms. Godfrey—
                but I'm just not sure we're equipped
                    to handle Selah's . . . situation.
                    Unless Selah can demonstrate
            that she can get through the rest of the year
                    with no more behavioral issues,
                        no more disruptions,
                and you can make a compelling case
                    for why she should stay,
            we will not be able to welcome Selah back
                        for the eighth grade."

I expect Mom
to wither, but instead
she turns tomato red.

"Well, you *were* equipped
since Selah's had no issues
until now. Selah's been here
since the beginning.
I thought Pebblecreek
was all about
investing in your students,
your *family*."

Principal Merkert squirms.
He knows my mom—and my poem—
are right.
"Of course we care
and want to help Selah
however we can.
We just think
it might be best for Selah
to transfer to another school,
another school with more resources
than we have here at Pebblecreek.
We think it would be
better
for *her*."

Not the Best Fit

What if he's right?
What if I *should* leave Pebblecreek?
I've been trying to have
"no more behavioral issues"
as it is, and have already failed.

It's not like I
want
to go,
but I don't think
Principal Merkert cares
what I want.

How can I
make them keep me
if no one
but Mrs. V and Noelle
wants me here?

Even if I follow
all my rules,
even if I write good poems,
nothing will change
the fact that I am different
and Principal Merkert
doesn't want
someone like me here.

The whole drive home,

Mom says things like:

"This school has known you
since you were a little girl.
Parents have always made sure
to include you
in parties and sleepovers.
They should know
you're anything but
unpredictable.
Why would they say that?
It just doesn't make sense.
I won't let them abandon us like this.
It'll be fine, Selah.
Everything
will
work out
fine."

But as her words
circle around each other
like birds, as she tries
to smile
but it doesn't come out right,
as she breathes fast
every time
a car comes close to her
on the road,

I realize
she's just like me.
Her rules
are failing
her too.

But Mom doesn't have
steam holes.

She's been so good
at her rules
for so long,
I didn't even notice
there were more words
waiting inside her.

But now
they're starting
to slip out of the cracks
like boiling water.

What if she boils over?

Crayon People

When I was little,
I used to only
draw with crayons.

I kept some in the cup holder
in the back of Mom's van
so I could always have them on hand.

But then one summer day
I put my hand in
only to feel
the hot melted wax on my fingers.

Maybe I was wrong.
Mom *is* like me,
and we are like those crayons—

we seem Normal and fine
until it gets hot enough
that we lose our shape.

More and More

The next day after class,
Mrs. V pulls me aside
and we sit at her desk, where her walls
are covered in posters with poems
I could spend all day reading.

"I'm sorry about your poems," she says.
"Principal Merkert didn't like them, did he?"
She lets out a huge sigh,
like she's been holding it in all day.

I think about telling her about the office visit,
how he said I'm "not the best fit" here,
but I bite my lip. Sharing the poems
was Mrs. V's idea and it only
got me in more trouble.

"In the future, he's asked that I stick
to the English bulletin board
unless we get permission in advance
and 'consider how the content might reflect on the
        school.'"
She shakes her head. "Every day,
it seems like there are more and more new rules."

I guess I'm not the only one
trying to figure out rules.

"It's not your fault, what happened," she says.
"It was brave of you, to be willing to share your work—
and I've heard the other students talk about it.
I think they relate to your poems.
Whatever you do, don't stop writing. We'll find
another way to get your work out there.
In fact, I think we'll have some more
poem assignments coming up
in the near future."

Mrs. V smiles, her eyes lighting up
so excited and bright,
like headlights in the dark
I have to look away.
I don't know
if it's that easy
to be brave,
if I can be as sure
as Mrs. V.

During cleanup time,

Noelle and I walk
with a tub of disinfectant wipes
to clean the banisters and doorknobs.

As soon as we're alone,
Noelle asks,
"Was that your poem, hanging in the hall?
Everyone's talking about it."
She elbows me.
"Way to call out Mr. S for being
a total jerk. It's about time."

"It wasn't meant to be about—
or just about—Mr. S.
He's not the only one
who makes me feel
like an outsider."

Noelle nods.
"That's true,
though you know
everyone thinks it's about him.
Did you know
he has a whole drawer of stuff
he's taken from students?
Now he's had to empty it
and give everything back."

I smile, cleaning
the front entrance door handles.
Even if Principal Merkert
doesn't like my poems,
even if he doesn't want me to stay here,
maybe my poems can still help people.

"Principal Merkert told me and Mom
we should consider going to another school,"
I say, my voice
barely squeaking out.

"What?" Noelle yells.
"That's so unfair!
Because of the poems?"

"He thinks I was being disrespectful," I say.
"But he missed the point.
I wasn't trying to hurt anyone.
I just wanted us to do better."

"I'll refuse to go to school
until he apologizes," she says.
"The whole class,
we can do a walkout!"

I look down at the sidewalk.
"The thing is . . .
what if he's right?
Maybe I'd be better
in a different school.
A school that has resources
for people like me."

Noelle gets quiet.

"Mom wants me to stay,
Pop wants me to go . . ."

"But what do *you* want?"

Even if I knew,
would it really
matter?

Do I Want to Stay Here?

In the morning on the way to school,
Mom says, "We can't let them push us out."

After school on our bikes, Pop says, "You can't stay
    somewhere
that treats you like week-old bologna."

We haven't had dinner together since Pop found out
since all they do is argue.

In my head, Noelle keeps asking, "What do *you* want?"

Nobody else has asked
what I want or need.
Mom and Pop talk
like I don't have any options.
But from reading online,
I know
there are lots of options.

I'm just starting to figure out how I work.
Wherever I am, I want it to be
a place I can speak
and get the help I need. But what
do I need?

Things I Learn Online:

1.

If I want to know if I'm autistic or not, I can get tested.

2.

If I need different things than my classmates, I can ask for
    something called accommodations.

Oh.
The more I read, the more I realize:
Mr. S should've asked about my tools.
But I shouldn't wait for him, or anyone, to ask.
I need to tell people
that my sunglasses protect me from headaches,
my earplugs make me feel safe and calm,
and my gummies keep me focused.

"We can't know what's in your brain
if you don't tell us," Mrs. V once said
when we were talking about one of my poems
and what it meant. I thought it was
so obvious
but she read it three times and had
no idea.
So I wrote and rewrote
until all my thoughts
became clear on the page.

3.

There are all kinds of schools out there,
different than Pebblecreek:
schools just for kids like me
schools with assistants
and computers that help you talk when you're wordless
and quiet rooms
and no uniforms

but also schools
with none of those things.

　　　　　　　There are schools that sound amazing
　　　　　　　　　　　but none of them
　　　　　　　　　　　are Pebblecreek.

4.

All schools—even private schools—have to follow laws that
　　　protect people who need help.

5.

Neurotypical:
neurologically typical,

　　　　　　　　　what I've always thought
　　　　　　　　　was "normal."

Neurodivergent:
people with variation
in their brains, people who might
be "different,"

　　　　　　　　　　　people like me.

　　　　　　　　Pop said we're in a world
　　　　　　　　　　not built for us,
　　　　　　　　a neurotypical world.

　　　　　　　　　　People like us
　　　　　　　　　are dragons
　　　　　　　with clipped wings,

　　　　　　　　but like Toothless
with his prosthetic tail fin,
　　　　　　　　we still find

　　　　　　　　so many ways

　　　　　　　　　to

　　　　　　　　　fly

Checkup

The doctor says I look healthy
and do Mom or I have any questions?

Mom says no, stands up to leave
and thanks him, but I have a question
burning in the back of my throat.

"Sometimes I get overstimulated,"
I blurt out. "I met someone who said
they're on the autism spectrum
and they seemed like me.
Could I be on that too?"

Mom stops in the doorway.
Smiles.
"I don't think
you have autism, sweetie,"
she says,

but the doctor takes notes
on his computer. "It's possible.
There are lots of people
on the spectrum, and plenty
who are undiagnosed, especially girls.
I can have the front desk give you
a referral to a specialist for a diagnosis."

"I don't know if that's necessary,"
Mom says. "There's nothing about Selah
that looks autistic, and she has
a perfectly normal life."

The doctor gives her a look.
"Autism manifests itself differently in everyone.
Sometimes the things people struggle with
aren't obvious on the outside."
He smiles at me.

"Whether or not you're on the spectrum,
this specialist can give suggestions
to help you manage your sensory needs
and help you feel less overstimulated."

I smile. "You mean like earplugs?
Those help me."

"That's great. Yes, there are lots of tools
and accommodations to help you
work *with* your environment
instead of against it
and live
your fullest, happiest life."

Mom's lips are still pressed tightly together
but she nods.
When we check out,
I hold the referral
tight in my pocket.
I bounce on my toes.
My story doesn't have to be
Selah vs. Everything.

Asking

I tell Mom about how hard it is
to sit through class all day
because our new chairs are so hard,
so she sews me a cushion
out of old pillowcases
to sit on.

I bring it to class
under my arm,
another thing that makes me stand out.
When I sit down,
it feels *so* much better!
I squirm less
and can focus through class.
Mr. S doesn't say anything
but I know he's happy
that I'm not squirming.

When I get up
to go to the bathroom between classes,
I come back to find Ezra in my chair.

"I was keeping your royal throne warm,"
he says with a laugh, then asks,
"Why do you get special treatment?"

"My mom and I asked to bring it in," I say.
"We got permission."

"No one else is asking to bring
fancy thrones in," Ezra says.

Mr. S doesn't say anything
but the way his eyes squint,
I know he's thinking
the same things Ezra's saying.

Geesh.

All this trouble
just over a chair cushion.
What will they say
if I ask for
all my accommodations?

"Fine"

On the way home from school,
Mom asks me how I'm doing.
I say fine, then realize
I'm saying fine because that's what the rules always said:
You have to say you're fine
no matter how you're feeling
because people only want to hear
"I'm fine."

Even though I know
my rules are made up,
I still keep acting
like they're there.

The rules live in my bones.
They live in Mom's bones too.

It's hard to tell
what are real rules
and what are my rules
from the way they grow together
like vines in a bush.

Mom nods
from the driver's seat.
"Good."
It's too late to take back the words.

Mom,
how do
you
feel
?

Rules

At Pebblecreek, everything is done the same way:
Girls' uniform skirts must be below the knee.
Clear nail polish only.
Wear no more than two bracelets at a time.
Earrings no bigger than a dime.
Only go to the bathroom between classes if it's an
     emergency.

I used to like the rules—sharp and exact
as if drawn with a ruler—
but they're exhausting too. I used to think
my rules could save me, make me happy,
but all I see now are the ways
they make me feel like I'm not enough.

After school on Friday, Mom talks
with my teachers and Principal Merkert,
trying to figure out how I can stay.

I've always been a Pebblecreek Kid.
It's weird to think about not being one.
It's scary to think about going through new, strange
     hallways
but it's also scary how every day
Pebblecreek becomes just a little more different.
All the possibilities circle my head like Hula-Hoops
and make my heart race.

I could stick my head in like a turtle
for the rest of seventh grade,
hope I don't explode,
eat in my classroom,
go to another school next year,
forget about Pebblecreek.
But what if I have to hide there too?
Noelle and Mrs. V wouldn't be there.
What if I couldn't find a single friend?

I'm tired of locking myself in a cave.
I want people to see
how beautiful ruby red my wings are,
how my fire burns warm and bright.
I want to fly.

I ask Mom

when we can schedule
the appointment with the specialist.

She says we'll see,
but days and weeks go by,
so I ask, "How soon is 'we'll see'?"
Mom narrows her eyes at me,
and I realize I must sound rude.

"We need to prove to Pebblecreek
that you can stay, that you are
just like any other kid there," she says,
all the words she doesn't say
hanging in the air between us.

But I'm not! I want to say.
I'm not just like any other kid.

Help

Kids at Pebblecreek get good grades
and get into good colleges.
I know Mom's thinking about this
when she says I *have* to stay,
that she doesn't want me to be left behind.
That she wants what's best for me.
But what exactly is best for me?

I don't know if Pebblecreek will let me stay or not.
I don't know if I care.
I'm not going to try to make them keep me,
but I am going to tell them what I need.

"Mom," I say,
"if I get diagnosed,
it might help me stay.
It might help them
help me."

Mom looks at me funny,
so before I chicken out,
I say
in the most adult voice
I can,

"If I stay at Pebblecreek,
I want accommodations."

Mom squints at me
like she's seeing something
she's never noticed before,
like a little sticker
in the window of a house
she's passed every day to work.

Finally, she says,
"What do you need

accommodations for, sweetie?
You're not
the kind of kid
who needs something
like accommodations."

So I tell her.

I finally make myself tell Mom

I hit Addie
because she was braiding my hair.

Because every pull stung
like there were bees
on my scalp,

and I tried to keep it all inside
but there wasn't enough room left.

That I know now
there's never enough room
to keep all my feelings inside,

and I can't keep doing
what I've been doing. I need
help.

Mom doesn't say anything
for a while,

then finally,
"I'm so sorry, Selah,
I'm so sorry I messed you up."

Mom Cries

"I tried so hard
to put on a brave face,

to keep you from seeing
my damage.

I didn't want you
to learn that from me.

I tried so hard
to make things normal for you—

I didn't know
what I was doing,

but I hoped so hard
you'd have the best in life.

I hoped so hard
I wouldn't damage you."

All I hear is:

My

                                                    damage.
Damage

                                                    you.

There   *is*   something

          wrong

                                        with

                    us.

Damage

Mom bites her lip.
She must see the

DAMAGE

on my face because she says,
"Oh no, I said
something wrong."

I feel around
my face
my brain
my pockets
for something clearly labeled
"damaged."

That's what
Addie's mom
and the other parents
would call me:

dangerous.
unpredictable.
damaged.

Like I'm some
mutant sea monster
that lives at the bottom of the bay.

Maybe Mrs. V
and the people at FantasyCon
were just being nice,
maybe I was right

to hide in my rules after all.

Without them,
I'm just a zoo animal

everyone looks at
from far away,
through a camera.
The kind parents
warn their kids:
Do not touch.

Thinking about it,
a sick feeling aches through my chest,
like the dragon inside me
is rolling around
with a bellyache.

but the part that hurts
even more:

Mom thinks
she's damaged,
too.

Set

I lock my bedroom door
curl up under my desk
and cocoon myself in heavy blankets.
Mom knocks, knocks, knocks,

says she's sorry,
says she knows she said something wrong,
says this is why she knows
she shouldn't say things
when she's feeling so much
because it always comes out wrong
and she ends up hurting others.

I know that feeling.
Mom, Pop, and I:
a discount-store toy playset
with missing pieces.
We don't do the things
you'd expect from the commercials.

Was my dad like this too?
Did words burst
in and out of him
like animals?
Was he
unable to set up a fence
between himself
and the world around him too?

Or is that exactly why he left:
because we were
too weird,
too damaged for him?

Love

It's almost time for bed
when I see Pop out the window,
walking up the driveway
to the house.

Through the door I hear Mom
in the kitchen
telling herself everything's
going to be OK
in that tired voice that says
everything's not OK.

I open the window,
stick my head out,
and yell into the dark,
"Pop!
Now's not really
a good time."

Pop stops and looks up at me.
He lifts his orange glasses.

The words pop
out of my mouth
like fireworks
before I even realize what I'm saying:
"Why don't you ask
before coming over?
It's rude to show up
without asking."

Pop frowns,
coming close to the window.
"We're family. You know
you don't have to ask
before coming over
to my house, right?

What's going on, kiddo?
It's not like you
to talk like that."

I shake my head.
I don't want to cry
in front of Pop.

But Pop is
a bloodhound.
He won't stop sniffing
till he finds what's going on.

"I liked your poem,"
he says.
"You're right.
I haven't always been
the most thoughtful person.
And that was wrong of me."

I frown.
I didn't expect that.

"It was brave of you
to write me that,"
he continues.
"You know,
your grandmother
was the only other person
who called me out
when I was being
a real dodo bird.
You got guts, kiddo."

I shake my head.
"I don't know
what I have, Pop.
Everything feels
all confusing
and messed up right now.

I don't know
what to do."

                                              Pop nods.
                                          Scratches
                                  his balding head.

"Why did
Dad
leave?"
I ask.
"Was it because
we're weird?"

                          "You know, most trains these days
                              are diesel or diesel electric
                              but no matter what you say,
                                      I will always love
                                      steam engines."

I frown.
"That didn't answer my question."

                                          Pop smiles.
                                  "What I'm saying is,
                                      people *change*,
                              often for shallow reasons.
                              The plane was invented
                                      and people
                              went away from trains.
                              Except for those of us
                              who really love trains.
                          When you love something,
                                      or someone,
                              you stick with them,
                  even if it's confusing or hard.
                              The people who don't
                                      are fickle
                          and not worth your time.

Also, I never liked
Donald. He talked
like a used-car salesman."

Outside,
the crickets in the dark.

"Did you ever tell Mom
that you love her like that?"
I ask.

Pop shoves his hands
deep in his pockets.
"Didn't I?
Isn't it
obvious? I said it
in everything
I did. I
love
that girl
to bits.
You think
I could live next door
if I didn't?"

When I don't say anything,

Pop says, "I'll come over
tomorrow, then,"
turns around,
and leaves.

Toss and Turn

Words inside me
like laundry
tumbling
forever.

The door to my mouth
locked
not enough quarters
to get them out.

Mrs. V would say
I should write a poem
about today.

Pop would say
I should write a poem
and also:
Forget what Mom said
because you know *we're not damaged.*
We're Godfreys, for crying out loud,
not cheap furniture.

We're Godfreys
through and through,
a different breed
and proud of it.

You and I
are cut from the same cloth.
We love
who we are. We love
what we love.

We're problem solvers.
Poets. Artists.
Change bringers.

Why settle and be
like everyone else?

But that's easy for Pop to say.

After Googling: Why Do People Call Other People Damaged?

People call people like us damaged
because we're different
because they don't understand
    why we act the way we do
because they feel bad for us
      and fear that we've lost something
      by not being like everyone else.

People call people damaged
because we need help sometimes
because we inconvenience them
because they assume we're unhappy
    that everything will be worse for us
    that we're a math problem that needs to be solved.

People call us damaged
because they think something's wrong
because they think we're dangerous
because they don't know
    what's really happening with us
because they don't ask
because they're afraid.

I want people to know
I am *not* damaged.
I am not a clearance item at an outlet store.
I am a *person*.

I want people
to read my poems
and understand who I really am,
without my Normal-person mask.

I thought I was damaged too
because that's what everything around me
        told me I was.
I don't have to believe that anymore.

(You don't have to either,
Mom.)

Poem for Mom

Mom,

Please don't call us damaged.
I'm not damaged,
and neither are you.
At least, not more
than anyone else is.

I know you're afraid
because I'm afraid sometimes too.
But I don't want to be afraid anymore.

You like me
the way I am
and I like you
the way you are—
isn't that
what matters?

I don't know
what it'd be like
to be like everyone else,
but I hate the idea
of feeling less
than I feel now.

Sure, I don't like
how loud sounds
poke like needles in my ears,
and I used to want it all
to go away,

but I love how the wind
makes me lose my breath
like a roller coaster
and how alive
the woods smell.

I love running my hands
on fuzzy blankets,
and the taste of good songs
humming in my mouth.
I love how much I feel
every time I write a poem.

Thank you
for standing up for me
at Pebblecreek.
I wish you'd say
what you're feeling more.
You might get the wrong words
sometimes
but so do all of us
and the people who love you
won't leave
over words.

Love,

Selah

I slip the poem

under Mom's door
when the lights go out
so I can go to bed
with my head empty
and relieved.

Waiting Room

The people in the waiting room
at the behavioral health center
look like anyone anywhere else—

There are people who flap their hands
and people with painted nails.
There are people in ties and dress shirts like my teachers
and people in T-shirts and shorts.
There are people playing handheld gaming systems
and flipping through magazines,
tapping their feet (like Mom, next to me)
and picking at hairs on their neck and forehead.

There are people with pink-white skin like me
and dark brown skin
and tan skin
and olive skin
and every shade in between.

There are kids my age
little kids
men and women Mom's age
people as old as Pop.

My doctor was right;
everyone looks different.
No two people are the same.

I'm not alone.
I'm not weird.

We're all just different.
We all just need a little help,
and that's OK.

After the appointment,

new books come in the mail
with titles like *Parenting Children with Autism.*

Mom hangs up nice thick curtains
that make my room pitch-black.

She brings home a weighted blanket
that both of us love to snuggle under
after a long, busy day.

Mom laughs, says,
"I didn't think it had a name.
I just thought everyone was like us."

Cleo

Pop is right
that people who love don't leave.
I know this
because despite everything,
I'm in Noelle's basement right now,
sitting in my sleeping bag,
trying to keep my eyes open.

I *want* to be here.
In the dark, Noelle
does her silly Sméagol impressions,
making us all scream and laugh
in our sleeping bags.

I want to get
to the quiet sleepover dark
where we whisper out
the deep things inside us
that we'd never say
anywhere else.

I want to start
sharing
what's going on inside me.

But Cleo's here,
so we don't get anywhere close
to quiet.

"You're so weird, Noelle."
She laughs.
"We should play
Light as a Feather, Stiff as a Board."

Noelle shrugs.
"That's a silly game.
It's not like anyone
is gonna float."

Cleo's lips scrunch up.
"You used to like it.
But whatever.
We could do a pillow fight!"

Without warning,
Cleo whacks me
with a pillow,
but it might as well
be a bag of concrete.

"Lighten up,
Selah!
We're here
to have *fun*,
not sleep."

Noelle's eyes get big,
watching me,
watching Cleo,
biting her lip,
wordless like me.

I run through my head,
gathering words in a net:
I'm tired.
Don't hit me.
You're so rude.
Why can't you shut up
and leave me alone?

But even though
I'm starting to find words
it doesn't mean
I can get them out of my mouth.

"You know it's a *game*, right?
Aren't you gonna
hit me back?
Or are you gonna give me
a bloody nose
like you did Addie?"

I wish I could find
my notebook in the dark.
I wish Cleo
would shut up
and never come back.
But whatever I do,
no matter how much she might deserve it,
I can't
hit
Cleo.

Noelle's face scrunches up.
"That's not OK, Cleo."

"What? It's a *joke*.
Can no one
take a joke?
I hear autistic people
don't know
what jokes are."

"What's *that*
supposed to mean?"

"Why do you even
invite her over, Noelle?
She doesn't even
like
sleepovers."

Suddenly,
the valve for my mouth
opens.

"Cleo,
if you think we're so weird,
then why do *you* keep coming to Noelle's?
Why don't you hang out
with your not-weirdo friends instead?
Or do you just make fun of them too?"

Cleo
doesn't
say
anything.

Noelle bites back a smile.

Inside my chest,
my heart is a train
at full speed.

We go to sleep
in uneven silence
but this time
it's not because
I broke down in the bathroom.

So I guess I'll call that
an improvement.

Letter

Another party next door.
So loud, I can hear it
even through my earplugs
and feel the deep bass beat
kick me in the stomach.

I know Mom would never let me
tell the neighbors to be quiet,
so when she isn't looking,
I write a complaint poem,
throw it in their mailbox,
and turn to run.

Brave

A woman walking her dog
stops me at the mailbox.

"Do you live here?" she asks,
her voice prickly like brush bristles.

My head starts up
a bunch of high-speed conveyor belts
with the rules I must've accidentally broken,
all the reasons she might be angry at me—

No.
No more of that kind of thinking.

I shake my head.
"No, I just was leaving a note for them."

Just like that,
her face softens
like chocolates in a hot car.

"You can't stand it either?
Those parties of theirs
keep me up all night."

"They bother me too
but my earplugs help.
Also, my mom got me new curtains
so I can't see the bonfire light.
But sometimes I can still hear
through my earplugs,
so I wrote a poem."

The woman smiles.
"A poem."

"It's how I find words.
I'm not always

good at talking.
And I feel better afterward."

The dog
pulls on its leash,
trying to chase
a squirrel in the yard.

"That's very brave of you,"
she says.
"Maybe your courage
will rub off on me
and I can talk to the other neighbors
and get this dealt with.
We're probably not
the only ones who feel this way."

Wouldn't that be great—
to not be
the only one.

Since I sent that poem,

it still gets loud at night.
Bonfire lights,
neighbor screams,
beer bottles glitter in the yard.

Poems don't change
everyone,
but that's OK. I said
what I needed to say.

The neighbor woman
called me brave,
but how am I brave
if I still haven't apologized
to Addie?

Poem for Addie

Addie,

I know I should've apologized sooner
but I was scared and embarrassed.
I'm really sorry I hit you.
I promise I didn't want to hurt you,
and I never want to hit anyone again.
I wanted to tell you
I don't like people touching me
without asking first. Maybe other girls
like their hair being braided
but it doesn't matter to me
if it looks nice or not
when it stings so much.

Selah

The rest of class,

my whole body is awake and alert,
dreading going to the other class,
going up to Addie,
tapping on her desk,
handing her the paper,
waiting for her reaction.

So after everyone leaves for lunch,
I slip into her classroom,
leave the poem in her desk,
grab my lunch bag,
and run downstairs.

Different

At the end of the day,
I feel a hand
scald my shoulder.
Then, as if realizing
it burns me,
the hand moves away.
I turn around.
Addie.

She looks at me,
her thick dark eyebrows
furrowed.

"What did you mean
when you said it stings?"

"What?" I ask.

"The hair braiding.
You said
it stings. But it doesn't.
It's just hair."

I frown.
"Yeah, it does.
I feel my hair
through my whole body.
Ponytails, braids, brushing, buns—
it pinches and burns and gives me headaches.
It pulls
like puppet strings.
You mean other people don't feel that?"

She shakes her head.
"I don't know," she says.
"I'm sorry. I didn't know
it hurt. Your hair

is so pretty. I was trying
to do something nice.
People usually like
stuff like that."

I frown. This whole time,
was Addie doing
all those annoying things,
trying to be nice?

"I mean, sure, I was confused
and freaked out when you hit me,
but Mom's been taking it too far.
I hope you'll stay
at Pebblecreek."

Even if Addie
can be annoying,
it's nice to know
she's on my side.

"Besides,
we haven't gotten
to talk much.
Why are you
so quiet?"

I can't help it—
I laugh.
As if it's not weird
how she talks
and talks
all the time,
a shaken-up,
overflowing Coke bottle
of words.

Addie and I:
two different people
who like

different things
and for once
I realize

there's nothing wrong
with that.

Cats

"You know,"
Addie says,
"I think you're like my cat.
She's really nice
until you pet her too much
and then she bites you.

She's not trying
to hurt you, she's just
letting you know
she doesn't want any more."

And I think
yes,
it's exactly like that.

She sighs.
"It's easy
with cats.
I wish
sometimes
people were like that too."

"Yeah," I say. "Me too."

Pop Comes to the House before Dinner

"I heard about your poems," he says.
"To the neighbors,
and the school. You know a poem's good
if it makes people feel things,
even if it makes them angry.
You must've said something
important that people didn't want to hear."

He hands me a box
with a shirt inside.
It says:

"You are a dragon.
Be a dragon."

Visiting Mrs. V

I tell her
I know
what might happen,
but I have
to make my case
for why I should stay
at Pebblecreek.
I want to share
my poems again.

In the middle of English class,

Mrs. V stops her lesson
and asks me if I would read
one of my poems.

My body goes tight
like a screw inside a wall.
Is this what she thought I meant
when I said I wanted to *share* my poems?

She smiles. "What if I read it instead?
Would that be OK?"

I nod. Maybe one day
I can read my poems
in front of my classmates,
the way I did at FantasyCon,
but not today.

She comes up to my desk.
I hand her my newest poem
and she begins to read:

My Case for Me

By Selah Godfrey

Even though I'm quiet,
I have so much to say

Every sound, touch, light
is a war in my body
that you don't see

I've been trying so hard
to be like you,
to follow
the rules for being normal,
but
I'm not

I am autistic

My brain
is different
but beautiful

I might be
the only one making
a case for me
but I know
if you make a little room
for my wings,
I'll fly

Some things are hard for me
that are easy for you
but I have plenty to contribute
like writing poems
and helping people with math
and being a good student

I feel
so
much—
I'm a puppet
whose strings
attach to everything:
the stuff sitting in our trash can,
the trees in our woods,
every noise from every room.

I'm a part
of everything,
I feel
all of it
like the whole world
is having a sleepover
inside my body,

but I realize now
I don't think I want
to trade that part
—or any part of me—
for all the "Normal" in the world.

When Mrs. V finishes,

a couple kids chuckle,
the same kids that chuckled
when she read the word
"autistic."
But everyone else is still.
They turn to me
but not like when I hit Addie.
Their eyes get big
and they smile.

They clap.

Will raises his hand and asks:
"So were those your poems in the hallway, Selah?"

I nod and say
they were.

When class ends,

Addie comes to my desk
and asks
if she can get a copy
of one of the poems
I had hanging
before in the halls.

"The one about the bugs,"
she says.
"I was gonna take a picture
with my phone,
but the next morning
I was sad to see it gone.
I can't stop
thinking about it."

It's a short poem.
I know it by heart,
so I take her notebook
and write it on the first page:

Different than Us

Funny how / bugs are / more scared of us /
than we are of them

but for some reason / we only feel better / once we've
squashed / all the bugs in our house.

When school ends,

I take my Case for Me poem
and hang it on the bulletin board
outside Mrs. V's office.

Principal Merkert will probably
rip it down—he might even
expel me,

but I don't want
to be afraid anymore.

What if someone else
feels the same way? What if reading
my poem helps them?

It starts

with one poem
next to mine
on the bulletin board
outside Mrs. V's office.

How did my other poems
get there? I wonder,
but then I look
and realize
it's not my poem,
but someone else's.

The next day,
three new ones.
The day after that,
five.

Every day,
Principal Merkert
pulls them down,

but every morning,
they grow

until Principal Merkert
can't keep up
and the mean red Sharpie words
get fewer and fewer
and the bulletin boards
can't hold all the papers

until the whole hallway wall
is covered
in poems.

Noelle finds me standing in the hall,

staring at the paper-lined walls.
"Let's see Principal Merkert
try to take all these poems down!"

I look closer at the papers and see
some of them have people's names
signed in the bottom corners.

On my desk, a note:

I'm sorry I didn't say anything

I didn't know you felt that way

Cleo said you were just trying to get attention or
  something and I believed her

But I like your poems

I hope you'll stay at Pebblecreek

You are courageous, Selah Godfrey

Mrs. V Was Right

At lunch,
people line the walls,
reading poems,
peeling back pages like scales
to read what's underneath.

Sometimes someone will tell
a friend they wrote this poem.
Sometimes they'll point to their favorite.
Sometimes they'll take pictures
and save poems on their phone
to read when they go home.

I can't believe
how many there are,
how many talk about things
I feel inside me too,
how many other kids feel
different.

Like I've never been
the only one
after all.

In the hallway after school,

while we wait
to talk to my teachers,
Addie's mom
marches into the office
in her designer boots.

It's impossible
to not overhear her,
demanding
to know why
I'm still here

but it's also impossible
to miss Addie's voice
jumping in,
loud as usual.

"Why *shouldn't* she stay?
Why do you not like Selah so much?"

"Well, sweetie, she *hit* you."

"She wasn't trying to hit me
and she apologized.
She's helped me with math
and she's my friend.
Aren't you being
pretty unreasonable?"

"Pebblecreek
is supposed to be
safe.
That's why I chose
this school for you.
It has *standards*.
But it's not safe if—"

"*Mom,*
Pebblecreek is only
unsafe
if you're scared
of kids
like Selah."

Addie's mom
doesn't say anything to that.
The whole office
goes quiet.
I don't think Principal Merkert
or anyone else at Pebblecreek
can say anything to that either.

My favorite part

of the *How to Train Your Dragon* movies
is when you see the new Isle of Berk
and there are all kinds of dragons
flying everywhere.
The people of Berk
stop being afraid of dragons.
The different dragons
look like bouquets of flowers
in the sky.
The thing I like about bouquets
is that good ones aren't made
of a bunch of the same-looking flowers.
The best ones have all sorts of different things
that when put together make something beautiful.

The dragon in my chest

is no longer caged up,
no longer in defense mode.

If you look closer at the dragon
you'll see she's made of poems.

She can spread out her paper wings,
share her word-covered scales,

relax her muscles
and just enjoy being a dragon.

Accommodations

Mom parks her car
in front of Pebblecreek,
pats down her hair,
then meets me at the entrance
and takes my hand.

Maybe I should be embarrassed
holding my mom's hand
like I'm three,
but in her hand,
I can feel her nervousness
collide with my nervousness.
Our same pumping blood,
warm and alive,
reminding me
no matter how things go today
we will make it through.

In Mom's wallet,
I found the folded tips
of the poem I gave her, snuggled in
right next to my baby pictures.
Right now, my poem sits
in her pocket
next to the list
she and I came up with
alongside my doctor
for what changes can help me—

a quiet space
dress code alternatives
computer use
my sensory tools
a switch from Mr. S's class—

if I stay here
or go to another school.

Mrs. V
agreed to join us,
said we're stronger
when we're part of a team.

In my pocket,
I've written out
the words I want to say
so I don't have to
fish for them in the dark.

In the hall
outside the office door,
Mom stops,
squeezes my hand.

I look up at her
and say,

"No matter what happens,
it's OK
if we need to cry."

Selah's NEW Rules:

- Fight for words, even if it's hard
- Don't assume people are attacking you
- Ask for help when you need it
- Don't wait to blow up
- Carry earplugs, a notebook, and a pencil at all times
- Remember, everyone needs a little help sometimes
- Don't stay afraid—do something instead
- Be honest and talk to people, even if it's scary
- Always, always write more poems
- And no matter what, don't be afraid to be a dragon

AUTHOR'S NOTE

I was always "different." When I was a kid, adults said I "marched to the beat of my own drum," and called my special interests in things like Pokémon "quirky." Even though I didn't speak until I was almost three, no one wondered if I was autistic. Instead, I was examined for hearing issues and assigned a speech therapist. I was an only child, living in a quiet home outside the suburbs, so I usually could recharge before getting overstimulated. Until I went to college.

In college, I was living with roommates, away from home for the first time. People were loud at all hours and didn't turn their lights off. I didn't understand—who *wouldn't* turn their lights off or need complete silence to sleep? I became overwhelmed, anxious, and had trouble sleeping for the first time in my life. I read a book with an autistic main character and began to wonder if I too was autistic. As I started remembering my childhood from a new perspective, and reading about others' experiences online, everything started to make sense. Autism helped explain how I work and how I can help my body work best in a world that often confuses and overwhelms me. When a therapist gave me a formal diagnosis, I—like Selah—finally felt like I had found my voice.

Autism is easily misdiagnosed and misunderstood, particularly in females. The original definitions and diagnosis criteria for autism were based on autistic males, but we now know that autism can look very different depending on gender. For females, sensory issues with food are often misdiagnosed as eating disorders. Our difficulties with sounds, touch, emotions, and social situations—anxiety. Many autistic females can mask and blend in with their peers, making others think they're "fine" or "just like everyone else." When I first started telling people I was autistic, I'd often hear something like, "You're too normal . . . there's nothing wrong with you." Autistic girls may have vibrant friend circles. They may make eye contact. They may keep everything inside instead of acting out, or focus on special interests that are considered more "socially acceptable" based on gender norms, like fashion or movie stars.

Every autistic person is different, but I hope Selah's story, and the thoughts shared here, help break down some of the assumptions and bad ways we talk about autism. Autism—particularly in people who aren't male—is much more complex and easily overlooked than we used to think. Like how Pop, Mom, and Selah are all on different parts of the autism spectrum, growing research shows that there is a genetic factor for autism. People my age and older have been nicknamed "the lost generation" because we didn't discover we were autistic until we became adults. Autism doesn't mean being good at math, a hermit, or nonspeaking (though it can). Autism is called a spectrum because it can have different colors, shades, and hues. There are certain elements that connect everyone on the spectrum, but how those show can look very different. For a fantastic article on this topic, I highly recommend NeuroClastic's "'Autism Is a Spectrum' Doesn't Mean What You Think."

An autism diagnosis doesn't have to be a "curse" or a "bad thing." I was so happy when my therapist diagnosed me. I *love* being autistic. My autism is what makes me love writing, and helps me deeply connect to my friends. Like Selah, I can't imagine being neurotypical. I don't *want* to be like everyone else. As my parents will be quick to point out, I have always prided myself on being different and a trendsetter rather than a trend follower. The way we talk about autism often focuses only on the difficulties, but rarely about the strengths we may have: focus, passion, care, honesty, consistency, a strong sense of fairness, loyalty. Autistic joy is real and should be celebrated!

If you think you might be autistic, I strongly encourage you to speak to your doctor. While there are lots of great resources online, qualified medical professionals will be the most helpful starting point for providing discernment and direction for next steps.

Resources

This is just a sampling of resources that I've personally found helpful or thought might be helpful for others. I hope you find some of them helpful as well. This is not by any means an exhaustive list; there are lots of great tools out there for autistic folks. Any issues with this list are on me. If at all possible, I strongly encourage you to explore this list with a trusted parent or guardian. For additional resources, visit: megedenbooks.com/selah-additional-resources.

Recommended Tools for Autism:

Some tools that I've found most helpful include: weighted blankets, weighted plushes, thinking putty, Koosh balls, earplugs, noise-canceling earbuds, fruit gummies, and stress balls. I find that communicating via text (some people use Augmentative and Alternative Communication [AAC] or apps like Emergency Chat) can be very helpful when I have low energy and become nonspeaking. If you get a weighted blanket, please make sure it is the correct weight for your size.

Recommended Books by Autistic Writers:

A Kind of Spark by Elle McNicoll

Get a Grip, Vivy Cohen! by Sarah Kapit

M Is for Autism: The Teenage Girl's Guide to Autism, and Everyone Else's by Vicky Martin

For even more great reads, please check out A Novel Mind's neurodivergent books database: anovelmind.com/database.

Other Resources:

NeuroClastic's article "'Autisim Is a Spectrum' Doesn't Mean What You Think": neuroclastic.com/its-a-spectrum-doesnt-mean-what-you-think

"Autism Myths and Stereotypes," Geek Club Books: tinyurl.com/geekclubbooksautismmyths

Autism Self Advocacy Network: autisticadvocacy.org

Autistic Girls Network: autisticgirlsnetwork.org

Autastic's List of Autistic Traits: autastic.com/women-autism-starting-point

Particularly for Adults and Educators:

A Novel Mind's "Neurodiversity/Autism Resources" page: anovelmind.com/neurodiversity-resources

Geek Club Books' list of resources for educators: tinyurl.com/geekclubbooksresources

Autastic's Apps for Your #AutLife: autastic.com/apps-for-your-autlife

Acknowledgments

Getting a book out into the world is a team effort, and one that reminds me how small I am and how big God is. I'm so grateful for all the incredible people He's put in my life to encourage me and advocate for this book.

I'm eternally grateful for my parents, who always saw my differences as strengths, not "problems." To Dad, who taught me to believe I could do and be anything with enough hard work, and for expressing genuine confusion as to why anyone would have any problem with hand flapping. Thank you for telling the parent who asked, "Does Megan collect buttons because the other kids in her grade do?" "No, she collects them because *she* likes them," and grinning with pride. To Mom, who never made a big deal out of my differences, even when others wanted to say something was "wrong" with me. Thank you for standing up for me, always treating me as capable, and teaching me the power of a good book. I know I never would've fallen in love with writing or books without you.

I don't know what I'd do without my husband, who is the #1 best ally in the world and my favorite human being and friend. When I go nonspeaking, he's not afraid to be my mouthpiece, and has been known to call out gamers online who use autistic as an insult by letting them know "my wife is autistic." Thank you for supporting me, and always encouraging me to take this writing thing seriously.

I'm forever indebted to Laura Shovan, who has always gone above and beyond to mentor and show kindness to me. Thank you for your incredible feedback on early versions of Selah, and introducing me to the worlds of middle grade books and novels in verse in the first place.

A special thank-you to my early readers and advocates: Kelly Bingham, Linnea Ramsey, Renée LaTulippe, Sara Andrea Fajardo, Julie Houk, Diane Mungovan, JC Welker, Kathy MacMillan, Deborah Schaumberg, Sarah Aronson, the middle grade Pitch Wars Class of 2020, the MG in 23 debut group, and everyone in Writer.com's 2020 Verse Novels and Children's Book Workshop. Thank you for encouraging me to keep going.

I don't know if I'd be here without Eric Bell, my incredible Pitch Wars mentor who *saw* Selah and chose her out of all the other submissions in 2020. Thank you for getting the story I was trying to tell, and helping me believe I could actually do this writing thing when I was in my lowest of lows.

I'm so incredibly grateful for Lauren Spieller, my literal dream agent! Thank you for believing in Selah and being such a fantastic advocate for her story. Thank you for encouraging me to let my neurodivergent self out on the page.

I am still over the moon that Selah got as incredible of an editor as Emily Seife! Thank you for your enthusiasm for Selah from day one, and your incredibly thoughtful edits that pushed her story to the best it could be. You are literally everything I hoped for in an editor. Thank you so much to the whole Scholastic team for helping get Selah's story out there into the hands of readers, especially Cassy Price, Janell Harris, Jackie Hornberger, Crystal Erickson, Jessica White, Priscilla Eakeley, Lizette Serrano, Rachel Feld, and Elisabeth Ferrari.

Thank you to everyone who shared kind words at the Pitch Wars showcase or the *Publishers Weekly* announcement of Selah. Every comment from a fellow autistic person made my day, and reminded me why I wrote this book.

And of course, thank you, God, for making me autistic! I wouldn't want my brain to be any other way.

ABOUT THE AUTHOR

Meg Eden Kuyatt is a neurodivergent author and creative writing instructor. She is a 2020 Pitch Wars mentee, and the author of young adult, middle grade, and poetry books. When she isn't writing, she's probably playing *Fire Emblem*. If she could be a Pokémon, she'd be Charizard. Find her online at megedenbooks.com or on Instagram at @meden_author.